Murda Season

Romell Tukes

Lock Down Publications and Ca$h Presents
Murda Season
A Novel by *Romell Tukes*

Lock Down Publications
P.O. Box 944
Stockbridge, Ga 30281
www.lockdownpublications.com

Copyright 2020 Romell Tukes
Murda Season

Lock Down Publications
Like our page on Facebook: Lock Down Publications @
www.facebook.com/lockdownpublications.ldp
Cover design and layout by: **Dynasty Cover Me**
Book interior design by: **Shawn Walker**
Edited by: **Leondra**

Stay Connected with Us!

Text **LOCKDOWN** to 22828 to stay up-to-date with new releases, sneak peaks, contests and more...

Thank you!

Submission Guideline.

Submit the first three chapters of your completed manuscript to ldpsubmissions@gmail.com, subject line: Your book's title. The manuscript must be in a .doc file and sent as an attachment. Document should be in Times New Roman, double spaced and in size 12 font. Also, provide your synopsis and full contact information. If sending multiple submissions, they must each be in a separate email.

Have a story but no way to send it electronically? You can still submit to LDP/Ca$h Presents. Send in the first three chapters, written or typed, of your completed manuscript to:

LDP: Submissions Dept
P.O. Box 944
Stockbridge, Ga 30281

DO NOT send original manuscript. Must be a duplicate.

Provide your synopsis and a cover letter containing your full contact information.

Thanks for considering LDP and Ca$h Presents.

Acknowledgments

First and foremost, I would like to thank Allah for his blessings. My readers and fan base, much love! Please continue to rock with me. Shout to Peekskill, my MGF team, Naya, Tank, mama luv, killer, Berty. My Yonkers fam Smoke Black, Fresh, Kazzy, YB, Lingo, Smurf, Spayhoe, Elm St, and CB. Can't forget about Baby James and King Hand, My Patterson, NJ team and Newark Blue, B.G., Beast, Rugar, Nap. My Philly squad Blazer Beast, Dime, and Big C. My BX crew Melly, Humpy, the twins from East Tremont, BJ from East Chester, P. Cod, my son Dru Burnoide. My Brooklyn Knights Tim Dogs, OG Chuck, K from Thompkins, Scrapp from Fort Green, Thug, Tails from Crown Heights, Gunnie, and my guy Black Knowledge A-Team. Free the real, Bomei aka Fatal Brim, and big shout to LDP. We got the game on lock stay tuned…

Romell Tukes

Chapter One
Tarrytown, NY

Stacks sat behind the tints of the parked Chevrolet Malibu watching the middle-aged white man dressed in a Canali suit, place his two daughters in the minivan along with a pretty white woman, who looked like model.

This was his every morning routine before leaving his mansion in Tarrytown, which was forty-five minutes away from his workplace in the city. Once the man sent his kids to school with his wife, he ran back inside his house to get his snakeskin before heading to work.

Stacks was checking his submariner Rolex as he saw the man pull out of his garage in a badass gray Audi A8 with curtains in the back windows.

"Perfect timing," Stacks said to himself as the Audi passed him. The driver paid him no mind as he was on the phone.

When the car was a good distance, Stacks pulled out of his parking spot to begin tailing the Audi, something he had been doing for three days now. Each morning, bright and early, Stacks would follow the mans every move, even at his place of business.

The man's name was Joe Mussari. He was the son of a federal judge and was a very successful lawyer who took on civil, criminal, and any type of business cases.

Due to his Jewish background and his father's ties, he was a very connected man. Unfortunately, he was greedy for money, just like any other Jew in New York. He loved spending money on anything, including golfing and random yacht trips. His love for spending money is why he had to file bankruptcy twice.

***

Hours Later

Mr. Mussari was drained. He spent the day in court defending one of his high paying clients beat a murder case.

He knew the odds were against his client but still pushed for the claim to go to trial, so the presiding judge, who happened to be his father, would have another conviction under his belt. Mussari hated black people, so despite his client paying him $125,000, he didn't care if his client was innocent but found guilty, as long as he was paid in full.

Once the office was closed and his coworkers were long gone, Mussari called his wife, Carrie to inform her he would be late getting home. He let Carrie know he was reviewing caseloads, but the truth was, he was looking forward to spending time with his mistress. Lying became something he did daily, but if he had to do so to see his side piece, then so be it.

He was rushing gathering all of his documents while searching for his car keys, so he could go to his her apartment. His mistress just so happened to be the wife of one of his clients.

"Slow down, honky," a male voice said, making Mussari jump back, almost falling over his chair. He was scared to death as he looked at the black man in a Michael Kors suit.

"Hey man, we're closed. We can take new criminal cases in the morning," Mussari stated, wondering how the man got inside. He knew he told his assistant to lock the front door earlier.

"This ain't that type of party," Stacks said pulling out a 50 Cal pistol with a long thick barrel.

"What's going on? I'm sure we can take about this. I can write you a check or whatever you want. I got kids man," Mussari spat out quickly.

"Sit down. I'm here on the terms of Web. He sent me to tell you the agreement is up. You violated the terms." Stacks tossed him some papers he had in his back pocket, which reflected the stolen money in Mussari's name.

Mussari was Web's lawyer. He handled all of his business agreements, contracts, lawsuits, and property contracts and Web made sure he paid him well. When Mussari read the paperwork, he knew he was caught red handed. He had stolen hundreds of thousands of dollars from Web for years.

"I can pay the money back. Please, just give me some time man. I'll pay double," Mussari begged.

"I'm sure you know it's never about the money with a man like Web." Stacks enjoyed seeing the man sweat like he ran a marathon.

"This wasn't my idea. It was Freddie, from the mob. They wanted me to shut down all of Web's operations. I didn't have that type of power, though so I had to do something, or they would've killed me." Mussari's eyes were filled with tears as he told the partial truth.

"Thanks for the story. I'll be sure to tell the boss," Stacks stated calmly before shooting him in the head twice, killing him instantly. Mussari's head was cocked back in his chair with revealing two bullet holes. Stacks left the office that was located in a shopping center and made his way to Queens to check on his shipment at his auto body shop.

Stacks was born Malcolm Sanders from Brooklyn, New York. The Brownsville area was where he grew up. His mother, Anna was a schoolteacher until the day she died, when Stacks was sixteen. His father was a deadbeat so when his mother passed, Stacks turned to the rough streets of Brooklyn.

After his mom died, he moved in with his grandmother in the East New York section of projects called Pink Houses. Pink Houses was known for a lot of criminal activity. He ran the streets and built a name for himself busting his gun but when he met Web at sixteen, his life changed.

Now at thirty-two-years-old, Stacks was a wealthy business owner and king pin in New York. He was dark skinned and stood six feet tall with a muscular but fit tone. He kept a low, clean cut but had deep waves. He was handsome, well spoken, classy, smooth, and was very smart. Never seeing a day in a cell was his key to success, so he picked and chose whom he dealt with wisely, being sure to avoid rats and snakes.

***

Queens, NY

It was nightfall and the snow was at least four inches thick on the New York streets. Winter in New York was like the north pole, but it was the one thing New Yorkers loved about their city. Stacks called it Murder season while most called it winter hoodie season.

Stacks pulled into his auto body shop to see a couple of cars on lifters and some were parked, waiting to get fixed over the next few days.

"Everything is everything," VP, one of his workers, said as he closed the garage door so they could breakdown the shipment that arrived two hours prior.

"Good. Everybody left, right?" Stacks asked climbing out of his Chevy he used for his dirty work.

"Of course. I sent everybody home early," VP said knowing Stacks kept a very low-key profile. He barely even came by his shop. Some of the workers never saw Stacks before. They thought VP was the boss.

Both of the men heard loud banging coming from somewhere. They were skeptical, knowing it was 10pm and customers knew the shop was closed.

"You hear that shit, son?" VP inquired.

"Oh damn, B. I forgot about this nigga," Stacks said as he pulled out his pistol with VP following suit. They both made their way to the back of the Malibu.

A black male in his twenties was tied up with duct tape around his mouth. You could hear him breathing heavily out of his nose. He trying to move but was unable to as he looked at both men with wide crazy eyes.

"You still don't know where my money at, Duke? I looked out for you and you still stole from me?" Stacks asked as the man started mumbling. "I'm sorry too," Stacks said shooting the man seven times then looking at VP.

"Huh?" VP was confused as to why Stacks was looking at him oddly.

"You not putting in no work? What, you tired?"

"You ain't even hear what the nigga was saying," VP said as Stacks closed the trunk. He regretted giving Duke thirty keys of coke. Duke ran off and it took Stacks nine months to catch him. Stacks caught him at four in the morning as Duke was leaving his baby's mother's house in Flatbush. He pistol whipped him and tossed him in the trunk on his way to Tarrytown.

"I heard him. I understand mumble talk. I listened to the Migos and Lil Uzi Verts," Stacks said making VP laugh. They walked towards the big blue van where the drugs were. "Get rid of that Chevy ASAP."

It took both men close to two hours to divide the five hundred keys of uncut fish scale coke with crystal flakes. They placed one hundred keys in five different cars and parked the cars in the lot outside, readily available for his clients to pick up the following morning. Once they were done, they dapped each other up and went their separate ways.

Chapter Two
Downtown Brooklyn

Murda looked over his shoulder at the clock, while lying in his California King sized bed. He was hoping he hadn't overslept. The morning sun brightened his bedroom through the crack of his Prada curtains his girlfriend, Erica put up in their apartment.

The crazy fuck session he had with Erica last night, had him not wanting to leave the bed, but he had a long day ahead of him.

Murda climbed out of bed to see his phone flashing, notifying him of missed calls. One was from his best friend, YB, two were from Erica, one was from his connect Sleepy, and two were from his mom, India, who most likely wanted money to get high.

He made a mental note to call them back later as he walked into the bathroom to take a shower and get ready for his day.

Looking at himself in the mirror, he smiled. He didn't have gray hair, or a bald spot in the middle of his head despite the rough nineteen years he had on this earth.

At age nineteen, Murda stood at six foot two, with a lean build, high yellow complexion, hazel eyes, tattoos covering his body, short curly hair, a thin mustache, perfect dental smile, and he always kept three slits in his eyebrows.

Murda was born Jamel Tyler. He born and raised in the Pink Houses in East New York, which was known for its violence, gang activity, drug infestation, and robberies.

Murda and his little brother Gunna, who was a year younger than him, were both crack babies, thanks to their mother India. India was the baddest red bone in Brooklyn until she got that monkey on her back.

Unfortunately, Murda never met his pops and India didn't know much him neither. She claimed it was one of those drunk nights where she forgot everything that happened. His brother, Gunna's father was murdered over a dice game in Mercy Projects, weeks after Gunna was born.

Growing up was tough on him and his little brother. Their mother was never around so they had to survive off Ramen noodle soups and grits for breakfast, lunch, and dinner.

The clothes they wore to school were old and faded with holes, but they never complained, even when kids would tease them.

As Murda got older, he jumped off the porch and started hustling in his projects and at school. Six months into selling dope, he got caught in high school with five small bundles of heroin, which landed him on Rikers Island for eight months, on the rough G-74 adolescent block.

There, he became a gang member of the Blood Nation and he received his GED. Erica used to have her older sister take her to see him, since she was only sixteen years old. That's were the two fell in love with each other.

When he came home from his bid, he dove headfirst into the streets with his best friend, YB, who was a trigger-happy hothead nigga. Once he met Sleepy two years ago, money began falling from the tree. He was making one thousand to two thousand dollars a day, which was cool with him. It was better than robbing or killing a nigga the Brooklyn way.

Last year, he moved out of his mom's house into apartment downtown with Erica once she graduated high school. Luckily, she worked at the hospital with her older sister, and she was in college part time, studying to become a nurse.

Murda took care of his little brother. He didn't want for nothing and he was the number one point guard in Brooklyn. He already had over ten division one colleges trying to recruit him. Once he was out of the shower, Murda went in his and hers walk in closet and admired his side filled with designer clothes and a variety of shoes such as Timbs, Air Max 95's and Jordan's. Erica's side had racks of dresses, shoes, purses, a variety of coats made by Bottega Veneta, Fendi, Celine, Off-White, Balmain, Dolce & Gabbana, Versace, Dior and so much more, because he spoiled her.

He grabbed a Rag & Bone outfit with a pair of tan butter Timbs along with a North Face coat. After getting dressed, he grabbed a quick snack out of the kitchen. He admired how neat and clean the place was because Erica had OCD and was a neat freak.

Murda left the apartment and hopped in his red and black Camaro SS, which he loved because how fast and powerful it was. He loved his neighborhood. It was quiet unlike Red Hock projects, which was located three blocks away.

Today would be his first time copping a whole brick of coke from Sleepy. He felt as if he was on top of the world as he sped through the Brooklyn streets on his way to Flatbush Ave.

***

Flatbush Ave., Brooklyn

Sleepy set at the table, weighing bricks and making sure each key weighed in at 1008 grams. He started doing this because his Dominican connect, Woody, shorted him two grams each key at the last drop off.

Luckily, Woody corrected it. If not, Sleepy was ready to start a war with Papi because he was a petty nigga.

"Damn, cuz. Niggas just got hit on Fulton Ave," Trap said reading a text he just received from one of his soldiers from over there.

"Nigga, that shit ain't got shit to do with me, son. You better post them dumb ass niggas bails before they start singing," Sleepy told his little brother who ran most of the Flatbush area.

Sleepy was in his mid-thirties. He been in the game for years. He was moving fifty bricks a week on a bad week. He was a short fat cocky nigga with a big mouth. He was Cripping heavy. Him and his brother trapped so both men were known throughout BK.

"That little nigga still coming. He passed ten grams yet?" Trap said, calling himself being funny, talking about Murda

"Son about to get a key today. He paid for it two days ago. He had to wait until I hollered at Woody," Sleepy said

"I don't know why you deal with him anyway," Trap told his brother as Sleepy stopped doing what he was doing.

"Nigga, this is my fucking operation. I do what I want. Just because you don't like him for some color shit, don't stop my paper. Everybody needs soldiers. He's the reason why we're moving in his hood. Son put on for the East so niggas respect him," Sleepy said, sticking up for the kid.

"Aight whatever but he got a bad little Spanish bitch. She needs to be with a real baller," Trap laughed although Sleepy wasn't.

Trap was a twenty- six-year-old hot head that was also Sleepy's enforcer and muscle, while suppling the hood with his brother drugs. He had a vicious gun game with a couple of bodies under his belt.

He had short man complex, standing five foot six inches tall, skinny, with long ASAP Rocky braids and two teardrops tattooed under his eye. He was always dressed in designer clothes and rocked a big Jesus piece on his neck, daring a nigga to rob him. Both men heard a knock at the door. Trap grabbed his loaded Draco off the couch and went to the door. Nobody knew of his stash house except for Murda. Sleepy trusted the kid. He took a liking to him when he first met him at juvie at West Indian Parcel in Brooklyn.

"You got company cuz. I'm out I'ma handle that situation and I'ma call you after."

"Aight, don't forget that bag for Rico and Cîroc on London Ave," Sleepy said pointing at the fourteen keys in the bookbag on the living room floor. "Murda, what's up, my G? How you doing playboy? Have a seat," Sleepy said as the front door closed.

"Ain't shit, just cooling," Murda responded wondering why Trap always got on some funny shit when he come around. The two never said a word to each other, but Murda never liked his vibe or energy.

When Murda was on the Island, Trap's name was ringing bells. He cut three big Blood homies in the face in the booking area each time. Word was he had a mean body count but Murda did too. That's how he got his name.

"That key is for you over there on the counter table and this is on consignment. Just give me the normal thirty-two bands," Sleepy said weighing his last four keys after handing him one.

"Good looks son. I got you," Murda said knowing he was about to be up, especially because the first of the month was approaching. He spent his last dollar on the key, so he was down bad but now he was back. The two talked for an hour before they parted ways.

**

King County Hospital

Erica was spending her lunch break in the café at work, taking selfies. With over ninety-five thousand followers, she stayed up on posting new photos.

However, with ninety-five thousand followers came thirsty niggas. Just today alone, she blocked sixty-five niggas trying to slide into her DM.

Erica Martinez was Puerto Rican and Dominican. Her mother was a beautiful Puerto Rican woman who worked in a hair salon for as long as Erica could remember.

Her father was a Dominican man who lived in San Cristobal, Dominican Republic, where he owned land and had another family. When her father Alex met her mom Julietta, they fell in love and had three kids. But, one day, seemingly out of the blue, Alex disappeared leaving a note telling her he was married with eight other children. Not one to waste her life, she moved on and raised her kids like a strong Latina woman.

Erica got most of her beauty from her mom. She was five foot five height, nice round, ample ass that was curvy and wide enough to turn heads, green crystal eyes, thick soft lips, C cup perky breasts, high cheek bones, perfect jaw structure, long dirty blonde color hair, flat chiseled toned stomach and most people think she resembled the actress Olivia Culpo.

Since she was done with her salad, she decided to head back upstairs. Erica was about to text Murda when she saw the blocked number. She already knew it was her brother locked up in the Feds.

After speaking to her brother, she sent him one hundred dollars via her Western Union App and then went back to work. She hoped he beat his RICO case he caught in Brooklyn this past summer.

Romell Tukes

Chapter Three
Manhattan, NY

Webster Jones aka Web, sat in his upstairs office in his lounge, called the Web Lounge, in the heart of Manhattan. His lounge was rated one of the best lounges in New York because of his big events and diversity of crowds. Web Lounge had two floors. One floor was Hip-Hop and R&B music and the second floor was Latina music and Rock 'N Roll Friday through Sunday.

Each floor had glass French made bars with high architectural designed crafted ceilings, four VIP sections with Ralph Pucci furniture, Fendi curtains for privacy, and wall to wall Bottega Veneta carpet throughout the lounge. Security guards stood on each floor just in case shit got out of hand and the most beautiful bartenders the city could offer worked in his lounge.

Web sat behind his two hundred twenty-five thousand dollar dazzling handcrafted desk, that was made in Paris, going over some business documents.

Web was born and raised in Cypress projects in Brooklyn. Growing up in a single parent household was regular. His mom was a strong, proud black woman who raised him and his brother Chris well.

When Web turned seventeen, he met a Dominican man who claimed to be his father. Growing up, his mother never spoke a word about the man who got her pregnant and disappeared like the wind. When he approached his mother about the man who claimed to be his father, she confirmed it, but she wanted nothing to do with her son's father.

After months of getting to know his father, Jose, he was kidnapped and killed by a notorious Cartel Family.

A couple of days before his father was found dead in DR, Web had gone to his father's apartment to let him know he had graduated high school with honors and was going to go to school to be a lawyer like they discussed.

Once in the house, Web saw a letter on the counter that crushed his dreams of having a father and son relationship.

In the letter, Jose told him he was an international drug lord. He let him know about a Cartel family that wanted him dead and he would most likely never see him again. He explained to him that this was the reason why he wasn't his in life growing up. As soon as Web was about to rip the paper up, he saw an address on the back telling him to be successful.

Web thought it was a joke, thinking it was just an excuse to continue to be a deadbeat until days later, his mother broke the news to him that his father's body was cut up and disposed of in his house in Dominican Republic.

Web was hurt a little because the time the two of them spent was like he knew the man forever. Web remembered the piece of paper with the address and took a cab. When he got to the address, he saw it was a storage place. Thinking he had the wrong address, he checked it again to see it was correct.

There was a number nine on the paper and a combination code to a lock. He went to the storage bin nine to see a huge lock on the shed. Once he put the code in, it opened. It was pitch black inside but when he turned on the light, he almost had a heart attack.

Web saw all white bricks stacked to the ceiling in rows and stacks of money in the other corner. Web locked the place up and left scared but excited. He went home and came up with some plans to take over the game and he did just that with the help of a crew from his projects.

Ever since then, Web never looked back. He became one of the most powerful men on the East Coast. He had a Columbian connect but he never touched drugs. He left that to his right-hand man, Stacks.

Web was a legit business owner and he carried himself like one. He was always in a suit, classy, well respected, and rich. His brother Chris was a federal agent. They didn't speak. At thirty-eight-years-old, he still looked twenty-five with a medium build, hazel eyes, goatee, clean cut, nice perfect teeth, six-feet tall, and handsome.

The women loved him, but he was single and happy. He had plenty of bitches, but he couldn't give himself to a sack chaser like most bitches were in his life. When they saw his Wraith, his jewelry, his expensive condo, and his way of living, they could get thirsty.

Web was planning to open another restaurant and club soon but in New York, the mob owned everything. A nigga had to get their approval to open up anything in Manhattan or it could be deadly. And the Feds could be very suspicious of the business operations of men like himself; men that moved with swag.

This was why Web would put shit in other people's name but he wasn't going that route no more. He was a Brooklyn nigga. He could care less about some meatball eating fat fucks.

***

Brooklyn

YB was waiting patiently behind the Navy-blue Honda Accord he had borrowed from one of his side bitches.

The Honda was parked in the Gateway Mall parking lot as the nightfall covered the skies, which meant it was YB's time to shine as he waited for a victim to come out.

YB was a true Brooklyn nigga with a bad chip on his shoulder. He was nineteen and angry at the world in a vicious robbery. He robbed so much it became a hobby more than his survival.

He was six feet, skinny, with long dreads, a chipped tooth, loud, beady eyes and dark skin. He was from the Pink Houses where his aunt raised him and older brother Tookie. Tookie was serving a bid up north for robbery.

Selling drugs wasn't for him. His best friend Murda, tried to give him drugs all the time instead of robbing because he knew Brooklyn was small. Karma was a dangerous game, but he refused. This is why be loved living on the edge.

Christmas came early, YB said to himself.

***

PJ was a dope boy from Flatbush. he was moving keys thanks to his connect, Trap. PJ was also a part of the Crips.

Today was his girl, Dora's birthday. He took her shopping and also bought himself a couple of Gucci and Balmain sweaters because it was getting cold.

PJ walked to his sky-blue Maserati Ghibli with tints and black rims on low pro tires.

"Brace yourself, nigga," YB yelled, rolling up on them in an all-black Champion corn head hoodie with a 9MM pointed at both of them. YB wanted to laugh too. He always wanted to rob a nigga while saying that, since he saw it on his favorite movie *Menace to Society.*

PJ left his gun in his car, something he never did but he figured he would be safe in the mall with wifey. Then again, it's Brooklyn.

"Please, today is my birthday," the pretty brown skin chick said, who resembled Kerry Washington but extra thick.

"I like this rope chain. Give me this shit, son. It's my birthday too." YB snatched his rope chain, breaking it in the process.

"Look cuz, just take everything," PJ said dropping his bags and putting his hands in the air showing his Rolex by a mistake.

"I will. I'll be taking this too." YB roughly took the watch off of his wrist. "Let me see your wrist, bitch." Dora now had tears in her eyes because she sucked and fucked PJ for years to get the Date-Just watch she was sporting.

Without hesitation, YB snatched her watch and patted both of them down with one hand while holding them at gunpoint.

"Oh, here we go," YB said pulling out a wad of money from PJ's Palm Angel distressed jeans.

"Come on, son. You got everything, B. Let us go," PJ said, while remembering the niggas face. He was gonna make sure he found him and put a bag on his head so one of his wolves would get him. What YB had just taken from him, was champ change. He had more jewelry and a lot more money in shoe boxes.

"Thank you," YB said respectfully before he shot both of them twice in the face. An old couple saw him running, as they hide behind a van praying for their life.

When they saw the Honda with no license plates burn rubber flying out the parking lot, they stood up to be nosey, only to see a male and female lying in a pool of blood.

The white woman screamed in shock. She had never seen something so horrifying. Her husband called the police. He felt that the female still had a pulse while the man was flatline with two holes in his skull.

The old man was a Navy veteran, so he tried to give the girl oxygen by giving her mouth-to-mouth. The EMS arrived right on time to save Dora's life, but PJ was dead at the scene. The old couple told the police everything they heard and saw but it wasn't good enough. A description of a black man in a hoodie running was a needle in a haystack so the cops didn't waste their time at all.

Chapter Four
Pink Houses Projects

At nighttime, the projects looked like nightmare on Elm St. It was so dark because all the streetlights were mostly knocked out and cameras didn't exist in this part of town.

With twelve tall skyline buildings, a playground, a front and back parking lot, a NYPD patrol booth that was always empty because police was too scared to work there. Recently, two cops were murdered by an unknown suspect that the police were still on the hunt for.

Unknown to the police and niggas in the hood, Murda and YB killed the two officers months ago because they was harassing niggas, beating niggas up, taking niggas packs, and frisking teenage girls just to get a feel and if anyone resisted or anything, they would plant drugs or weapons on them and arrest them.

Normally, there was at least a murder every week in the projects. Especially when Tookie and Face were out because they were beefing with half of Brooklyn. When niggas would come through looking for them, they would be leaving out in white sheets.

Murda loved his hood. Him and Tookie brought everyone under their Blood set, so the whole projects was Bloods.

This is where Murda sold his drugs, but he had four workers who were the same age as his brother, Gunna. Murda could go in any hood in East New York and Bed-Stuy to open shop because of who he was.

It was cold out tonight, but that didn't stop niggas from shooting dice in the lobby buildings, drinking Henny, smoking loud, and posting up selling drugs.

Murda and YB were sitting on top of the bench in front of building fourteen, both in Timbs, hoodies, peacoats. YB was on the phone with Tookie, yelling, talking shit, feeling loose off the Henny.

Murda was thinking about the conversation he had with Erica this morning. She was telling him how she wanted a baby. When he told her that he wasn't ready for a seed yet, she went crazy on him. They ended up having a big fight, causing him to walk out while she was throwing shit at him.

"Yo blood. This nigga sends his love, but guess who just hit the spot with him?" YB said standing up with his new rope chain, Rolex, and clothes he stole from PJ.

"Who?" Murda responded although he wasn't in the mood to talk about jail niggas.

"Dre's bitch ass. I been trying to find this bitch ass nigga for years. Bro said he caught a drug case in Harlem and got a fresh ten piece. Karma a bitch. I did two years for that rat ass nigga." YB thought back to three years ago when he got caught at a lit basketball tournament in the East with a pistol. At the time, Dre was with him and got arrested also but as soon as Dre hit the precinct, he wrote statements on YB.

After Dre snitched, he moved to Harlem with his baby's mother and sister out of fear.

"So, what Tookie say?" Murda asked seeing his mom, India sneak in building seven. Since he gave her $1,000 earlier this morning, he hadn't seen her. She supposed to pay bills and buy food for her house, for her and his brother but the way she was moving, he knew he was up to no good.

"Tookie said he's going to shoot that nigga, Skrap. It won't fuck with his time because he's maxing out," YB said as he saw Murda get up with a look in his eyes. YB knew Murda better than himself. The two had been close since the sandbox. He trusted him with his life.

30

"I'll be right back," Murda said walking off through the projects as niggas was posted up. He bypassed everyone who sat around talking to hood rats, trying set up a late-night sex date.

***

India Tyler paced back and forth in the dirty, dark, pissy smelling third floor staircase waiting on Real, who was a middle age crack dealer.

India was thirty-nine and still beautiful. She was high yellow, with green eyes, a petite frame, thick juicy lips, long hair she kept in a ponytail, perky small breasts, flat stomach and good teeth with small yellow stains that Colgate toothpaste could make disappear.

Gunna was spending the night at his girlfriend's house and he had a big basketball tournament tomorrow. India knew she had all weekend to get high and do as she pleased.

Murda gave her $1,000 early for bills and food but she spent all of that on crack. Her lights were off, and her freezer was empty, and the cabinets were just as bare.

"Bout time. Come on, Real. I need you. I've been spending money with you all day. Fuck with me this one time. I need a twenty," she said looking at the Husky man with her puppy dog eyes as he closed the door behind him.

"India, I can't. I got to re up. This my last twenty," Real lied, flashing a nice size rock in her face, making her mouth water.

"I'll do anything."

"Anything?" he asked, grabbing his dick. She knew what he wanted. She would only do this when she had fallen on hard times. This was one of those times.

India licked her lips, got on her knees and pulled out his average size dick as he moaned. She didn't even lick it yet.

She traced her tongue around the tip of his head then she wrapped her warm, thick lips around his whole dick, sucking it up and down.

"Ummm shit." Real moaned. He heard her head and pussy was like that, but she had to be down bad, so tonight was his lucky night.

She worked his cock in and out of her mouth, deep throating his dick making loud slurping noises. He pushed her head down on his dick as he fucked her mouth like a criminal as she took it like a champ.

As soon as he was about to nut, he heard a noise behind him. Before he could even turn around, Murda's pistol slammed into his skull.

"What the fuck is wrong with you?" Murda screamed, with fire in his eyes as he pistol whipped Real. He continued to beat him senseless.

India was scared shitless. She only had one thing on her mind and that was the piece of crack that flew near the doorway. She crawled to get it and ran off as Murda was still pistol whipping Real.

When Murda saw Real was barely breathing, he shot him five times in the upper torso for the disrespect of having his mom suck him off.

A nigga ran in the stairway. He was Real's little brother. He was holding a small .380 special in his hand. When he saw who it was standing over his dead brother, he hesitated. Murda was his big homie.

"Do it, little nigga. I'll lay your ass right next to that nigga," YB stated sternly as he had a pistol to Real's little brother head

"I ain't see nothing," the little nigga said. YB still shot him in the head. He didn't like leaving witnesses. YB followed his boy in the building. He knew Murda was about to do something and he was always going to back his homie.

"Let's go," Murda state, running down the stairs leaving the building and jumping into his Camaro SS. He had to clear his head, so he went to the nearest bar to get a drink.

Romell Tukes

Chapter Five
Lower Eastside

Chris Jones sat in the basement of a custom may suit clothing store, owed by the Brooklyn mafia. The basement was a gambling room and a number spot to place bets with the bookies for sports events. It was smokey and dimmed.

Chris took a sip of his dark liquor while looking at his poker hand. Boom, the other foreman sat around the round table smoking cigars.

Everybody had their poker face on so Chris couldn't tell who had what, but he was down five thousand dollars already and if he lost his hand, he would be down ten thousand dollars.

Unfortunately, he only had two thousand dollars in poker chips. He lied about what he had in order to get into the game lien, by saying he had five thousand dollars because that was the fee to enter. Everybody in this room was wealthy men. Everybody except Chris, who was not only the brokest, but the only black man.

Looking at the full house in his hand, he was confident he had a winning hand. It would place him even with what he owed for today.

"I fold," one of the men said, pissed.

"Me too," a fat man drinking Brandy chimed in.

"I got two pair," Sammy said smiling, showing his yellow teeth. He looked at Chris and Freddy who were the family cops and most dangerous men in the room. Chris laid his cards on the table, smiling.

"Full house, gentlemen," Chris said knowing he won. He reached for the chips on the table, almost spilling his drink on his Talia suit.

"Hold on there, blacky…straight flush kid," Freddy said placing 4, 5, 6, 7, 8 in hearts on the table as Chris started sweating

"Good game. Chris your down ten racks. Where are your chips?" Freddy asked as people were starting to come in and out it was a busy night.

"Fred, can you put it on my bill? Times are hard right now. You know I'm good for it," Chris said nervously, knowing Freddy was vicious about his money.

"Chris, you came down here with no money and use your face to get in the game for the third time. Me and my guys take that highly disrespectful," Freddy responded strongly, smoking a cigar leaning back in his chair.

"I'm sorry, Fred. I mean no disrespect," Chris stated

"Aight, Chris. I'ma put it on your bill, but you're banned from down here for a month and now you owe $140,000. Get the fuck out of here," Freddie said as Chris grabbed his coat. "Leave the coat."

"It's cold outside, Fred. Come on man," Chris whined.

"It's going to be even colder if you don't pay me my money, nigga. Now get the fuck out of here," Freddy shouted getting mad.

Chris left the gambling spot and hopped in his Infiniti QX50. He headed towards his Westchester home with his wife and kids to prepare for work the next day.

Chris was a federal agent, but he was a dirty agent. He would steal from drug dealers, get rid of the evidence for the mafia, charge drug dealers and tax them for selling drugs a monthly fee or he would arrest them and their crew.

He was raised in Brooklyn by a single mother. His father was never around. All he knew was he was a black man who moved to Texas and died of cancer.

Growing up, him and Web had a good brother bond but when he went to college to become an agent, Web somehow got rich overnight and he became jealous. When their mom died, shit went downhill with the two and they hadn't talked since. That was five years ago.

Chris married a beautiful Italian woman who was the Goddaughter of Joe da Don. Joe was the boss of the Brooklyn mafia and was also a very connected man. Thanks to his wife, he became close to the mob and he did little jobs for them But that was mainly to clear his debts because Chris had a very bad gambling habit it was his drug and to make shit worse, he was an alcoholic.

Chris was forty years old, with a perfect trim beard, low cut, brown skin, smooth skin, hazel almond eyes, tall, lean, handsome and he had a very charming personality.

He had two daughters with his wife, Chelsea, ages six and nine. During his drive to his White Plains home, he thought of a way to pay Freddy his money.

**

Manhattan, NY

Jamika Astley sat at her desk working overtime tonight. Her boss brought her two big caseloads from the Bronx he wanted to indict before Monday morning, giving her less than forty-eight hours.

Jamika has been part of the bureau for almost four years. This was the only life she had.

She was twenty-eight years old with two college degrees, her own house, own car, own money, was single with no kids, and was a workaholic. She had a pretty golden skin complexion, was short and thick with big DD breast. Her body was toned thanks to her daily exercises. She had long curly jet-black hair, thick pink lips, neatly arched eyebrows, nice white teeth and dark eyes.

She was mixed with black, Indian, Guyanese, and Japanese. All the men in the borough tried their hand because she was so exotic, but she always declined respectfully telling them she didn't mix work with pleasure.

Jamika had a type and white boys weren't it. She liked strong black men. She wanted them to be independent and educated with a little thug to them because she hated a punk. Even though she could protect herself, there was nothing like a man's protection.

She grew up in the Bronx Uptown on Gunhill Road but now she lived in a brownstone house in Brownsville, only minutes away from the ghetto. She kept her life private. She had a couple of girlfriends she would go out with from time to time but that was the only fun she had.

After two hours, she was done typing up warrants for a crew of Crips from East Tremont in the Bronx. They were selling drugs, having shootouts in the broad daylight, committing both attempted and actual murders, as well as robberies.

She looked at their ages, seeing they ranged from eighteen to twenty-two-years-old. It was said that as young as they were, they were about to get hit with RICO charges and ten other counts that could land them in prison for thirty to forty years, if not more.

Once she was done, she went home and used her eight-inch vibrator until she squirted everywhere and went to sleep, just as she did almost every night.

***

Auburn Maximum Prison

Tookie was in the weight shack outside in the yard of the prison lifting four hundred and five pounds for his tenth rep on the flat bench with his work-out crew.

It was snowing outside but that didn't stop the prison workouts. Especially for Tookie, who was the biggest nigga in the yard standing a six foot four and weighing in a three hundred and ten pounds of all.

He was doing a three-year bid for robbing a nigga in front of a CVS. An hour after the robbery, the nigga he robbed was riding around in the black seat of the police car pointing fingers at Tookie.

Since Tookie had a crazy rap sheet, he took a three-year bid up north. Tookie looked just like Tookie the Crypt from Cali with big muscles, long braids, his cocky demeanor, brown skin, and very violent. The only difference was, he was a Blood gang member like everyone in New York.

"Hold the spot down son. I'll be right back," Tookie said as he stood up from the bench. He was dressed in his green state pants and a red sweater with workout gloves.

Tookie walked towards the two cut up niggas doing pull-ups at the bar near the gate.

"Yo, Tookie. What's popping big homie?" BJ greeted him. BJ was a Blood from the Polo Grand section of Harlem.

"What's poppin' homie?" Tookie stated in his deep voice while staring at Dre who just got off the pull-up bar. BJ got the fuck out the way. He saw Tookie put in a lot of work in the jail and it wasn't a pretty sight.

Dre know there was something funny about the big nigga who was lifting weights with the four Brooklyn niggas in the corner.

"Tookie, damn. What's good, my nigga?" Dre said putting on his hoodie and walking towards Tookie to embrace him trying to feel his energy.

At a fast and swift motion, Tookie spit a blade out of his mouth and cut Dre on the right side of his face from ear to lip causing blood to squirt in every direction. Tookie followed up by hitting him with a powerful right hook, knocking him clean out.

Tookie walked back to the bench and started lifting weights as everybody stood around in shock. Minutes later, the CO's came running from every direction and busted in the lock cage.

The officers handcuffed Tookie and took him to the box until he would be shipped to another prison since that was his third cutting in six months.

Chapter Six
One Month Later
Lil Italy

"I fucking told you, Vinny. I wanted that place. I had big plans for it and now you're telling me someone out bid me? That's impossible. I'm one of the richest men in this city. It better be Donald Trump who got the place," Joe said sitting in his office on fire, talking to one of his lawyers.

"I don't really know what happened because the investor's said you had it weeks ago but whoever the buyer was, must of been someone of royalty," Vinny stated with his legs crossed sitting across from the mob boss.

"Well at least we still got the property downtown on Madison Ave. How come you didn't bring the documents for me to sign?" Joe asked, lighting another Cuban cigar.

"That's what I was trying to get at, Joe. The owners just informed me that someone recently brought the place for a million and a half dollars, including paying for the foreclosure lease to seal the deal," Vinny notified him, hating to be the bearer of bad news.

"What the fuck are you talking about, Vinny? How is this even possible? This is the same owner, correct?" Joe snapped.

"Yes."

"Somebody was willing to pay basically almost two million dollars for a quarter mill worth of property and the location ain't even worth that much money," Joe said to himself, in deep thought.

"If I may correct..."

"No, you may not," Joe cut him off. "Somebody is playing games with me. Find out who brought the location.

41

Better yet, Vinny, I'ma have Freddy take care of it. You're fired. Close the door on your way out," Joe said picking up his phone to make a call as Vinny left.

Joe Goadagnicno was seventy-two years old, skinny old man with gray hair and glasses. He wore the most expensive suits money could buy. He was the number one Godfather on the East coast. He was a wealthy businessman, owning over nineteen business in the states.

He was original from Verona, Italy where he has a large family, but he was raised in Brooklyn, where he built his legacy.

Joe had plans to open a new Italy styled restaurant and an Italian shopping food center, but someone cut his throat. He was about to make it his duty to find out who this rich, white cracker is who was trying to step on his toes. When he found out, it wasn't going to be nice.

Joe was 100% legit but his capo, Freddy was the drug connect. He sold heavy weight throughout New York and Joe didn't mind, as long as Freddy gave him 25% of his network. The Mafia was against selling drugs, but Joe was a different Mob boss.

***

Pink Houses Projects

Murda was on the curb trying to get in his car so he could go back home to drop off the money he just picked up from one of his workers in his Gucci backpack.

He ran outta work and he been calling Sleepy for two days to only get his voicemail. This was regular shit every time it was time to re-up. Murda hated missing money.

It was sunny but cold outside today and Murda only had on a Versace sweater and skull hat. He left his coat at home because he didn't plan on being outside too long. He just had to pick up the rest of his money to go with his re-up.

An all-white Lamborghini, with snow tires was parallel parked next to his Camaro, blocking him in. He was starting to get impatient. It was ten in the morning. He wondered who was coming through his hood in a Lambo. Rappers were too scared to come to the hood, so he had no clue.

Two minutes later, a man wearing a tailor-made suit and a Tom Ford peacoat, was making his way to the Lambo. It was early so he wasn't worried about tickets.

"This you, fam?" Murda asked the man as he approached the Lambo.

"Yeah, my bad, son. I ain't mean to block you in. I was in a rush," Stacks said as he already knew who the young man was. He heard a lot about him through the grapevine.

"It's cool. You look familiar. You from around here?" Murda said checking out the man's attire, very impressed.

"Yeah, I'm from the back building, building eight. Your name is Murda, right?" Stacks said surprising him.

"Yeah."

"Look, it's nice meeting you, dog, but I gotta roll. When you get a chance, hit my line, son. I want to holla at you," Stacks said reaching in his coat pocket to hand Murda a card with his personal number on it. He was in a rush to attend a meeting with his worker, Woody.

"Aight, but what's your name?" Murda asked looking at the man bust down diamond Rolex, diamond rings and two heavy link diamond chains

"They call me Stacks. Take care and hit me." Stacks climbed into Lambo and pulled off. He was only there to see his baby sister, Sondra, to give her the ten bands he gave her each month.

When Murda heard the man's name, he was overwhelmed. Stacks' name in Brooklyn was heavy. Word was he was the richest and deadliest nigga in the city.

Murda used to always hear dealer dudes talk about the man as if he was a GOD or a Bumpy Johnson.

Murda placed the number in his pocket and hopped in his car, thinking about his encounter with Stacks. He liked the man's style.

***

Three Days Later

Murda contacted Stacks and both men agreed to meet up in Coney Island at a Jamaican restaurant. Murda walked into the medium size restaurant to the smell of curry chicken and ox tails cooking in the back. When he saw Stacks sitting in the back near the soda machine, he passed the small line of people waiting to order their food.

"What's going on? I like that Ferragamo outfit you put that together, "Stacks said admiring his style.

"Thanks."

"You tryna eat?" Stacks asked as he turned off his phone. He never talked business with his phone on just in case it would record. Smart phones were dangerous.

"Nah, I'm not heavy on Jamaican food at all. That shit runs through a nigga."

"Facts. Down to business though. I've been watching you for years. You move smart and you keep your circle tight. You're also not scared to put in work. I like how you did them pigs. A lot of niggas ain't got the heart to do that," Stacks said as Murda was shocked he knew about that situation. Stacks was in the parking lot that night coming from dropping off money to Sondra. He saw the whole shooting.

"I just try to stay focused on what matters," Murda stated as Stacks nodded his head slowly

"I'm a legit man, Murda. I own businesses but I'm also the plug and I need good, loyal men like you on my team. I don't fuck with too many people because most niggas is rats, snakes or hyenas, but I don't see none of that in you," Stacks said.

"I'm a different cloth."

"How many keys are you moving?"

"Two."

"Do you think you can move twenty?"

"If it's good but I don't have enough for that. I can only..."

"I'ma give you ten on the arm at twenty a piece and the other is for you to get on your feet," Stacks cut him off. Murda got cotton mouth. It was like a dream.

"Aight that's cool," Murda responded, trying to not show his happiness.

"Whoever you're dealing with now, let them know it's over, but you apart of the family now. Our business is our business. Keep it private, even from your friend, YB. I know he's loyal to you, but just keep your grass cut." Stacks gave him a piece of paper with an address on it before he stood to leave. "Merry Christmas." Murda couldn't believe he had a real plug now. Ironically, Sleepy picked up the phone this morning telling him to come by and see him, so he could hit Murda off with some work. Now he wanted to go holler at Sleepy to pay him his money, so he sent him a text to meet him at the fair in Coney Island.

***

An Hour Later

Sleepy pulled up to the packed theme park to see kids, parents, and teenagers having a good time. The winter snow was melted, and the sun was out today. It's what they would have considered, a warm Christmas.

When Murda saw a black GMC pull up next to his Camaro, he tried to hold his smile from his new business deal. He knew his life was about to change.

"What's shaking, boy? Why you call me way out here? I hate these corny Island niggas, son," Sleepy said hopping out the passenger's side, leaving three goons in the truck.

"My bad. I was out here so I figured you wouldn't mind but here is everything. I'm paying you in full for both keys so that's $64,000," Murda said, handing Sleepy the Gucci backpack as Sleepy looked confused

"One of those keys were for you, homie," Sleepy said wondering if he was slow.

"I know but I'm good. I found a new line so I just want to clear my face."

"I can never be mad at a nigga getting out the game," Sleepy said tossing the bag in the window to his driver. He was upset that he lost a good worker.

"I'm not getting out the game. I found a new plug," Murda said. Sleepy's facial expression went sour.

"What, nigga? You going cross me like that? Cuz this shit work like that," Sleepy shouted so loud, civilians started to see where the commotion was coming from.

"Keep your tone down, my nigga. I ain't cross you. I just found a better lane for myself. It's no disrespect," Murda stated as Sleepy laughed and hopped back in his truck

"I'ma see you around, cuz," Sleepy said as the truck speed out the lot.

Murda took that as a threat and now, he was pissed. He knew Sleepy took his humbleness for a joke, but now it was time to show him why his name was Murda.

Romell Tukes

Chapter Seven
Downtown Brooklyn

YB was in club Litty next door to club Lust. The place was packed with ballers, dancers, bartenders and grimy Brooklyn niggas with YB being number one.

Normally, YB would be in here to catch a victim but tonight he was there for another reason. He was posted in the VIP section with four of his goons drinking and smoking heavy blunts of weed.

Six dancers were on one stage twerking, pussy popping and sliding up and down on the pole.

"Yooo!" YB called a pretty bartender over. She was wearing cut off booty shirts, showcasing her big ass and flat stomach. Her liposuction surgery scar was light and below her panty line, but faintly visible.

"Hey, YB. What's up?" She knew who he was and although she knew he was bad news, she couldn't help but think he was cute.

"Let me get two bottles of Henny, the expensive *Paradis Rare* and two bottles of Louis XIII. You heard," YB shouted over the loud Young Thug music.

"Okay".

"You see that dark-skin chick over there dancing on the goofy nigga by the bar? Tell her to pull up," YB said as the bartender sucked her teeth. She didn't fuck with the stripper bitches. They were thirsty and grimy. There was always a bartender and stripper war in the New York clubs because the stages were behind the bar so the dancers were interfering with the bartenders tips.

Ten minutes later, she came back with the bottles and gave him his fifteen hundred-dollar total. YB gave her two bands. She was so happy she went and got the dancer bitch named Blossom, for him.

"Somebody called for me?" Blossom questioned, looking in their VIP to see bottles and hella weed flowing. It was her type of party.

"Yeah, have a seat ma," YB said as she walked past his niggas, being sure to put her big black ass in their faces.

Blossom was a tall, dark-skin older woman with a big huge ass and big breast that sagged from breast feeding three kids. She wore make-up caked up on her face, a weave, and high heels.

She wore a lace two-piece G-string outfit with her dark pussy lips hanging out the side as her ass swallowed the G-strings.

"Time is money cutie. Let me get some of that," she said sitting on his lap, while reaching for the bottle of Henny.

"Hooooldd on," all of his goons yelled, racing to get her a plastic cup because she looked like she was trying to drink out the bottle on some ratchet shit.

After she got tipsy, she was in the VIP twerking and bouncing one ass cheek at a time while making sex faces to all of them. She was down for a train, but tonight wasn't that type of party for YB.

"Let get out of here and go to the hotel," YB whispered in her ear as she was grinding on his hard dick.

"You got money, nigga? I ain't that drunk." He pulled at a wad of blue faces as her eyes widen. "I'ma go get my purse and get dressed. I'll meet you in the lot," she said strutting out the VIP as her ass was clapping.

"Yo, blood. You on some bullshit boy," one of his niggas said as he stood to leave.

"Next time. I'm hit y'all niggas later" YB said tucking his pistol in his low back.

***

"Ughhhhh," Blossom screamed as YB was ramming his hard twelve-inch dick in and out her wet, yet loose pussy as her legs were in the air.

YB was long stroking and pounding her pussy out. She was trying to run as if she couldn't take all the dick.

"You were talking hella. Shit take this dick," YB said pushing her legs behind her head as her face looked like she was in labor

"Ohhh! Yesss. I'm cummingggg," she groaned as he continued to air her pussy out. He started to smell a strong pussy odor of musk.

Once he nutted on her stomach, he bent her over started fucking her from behind as he grabbed her love handles.

Her ass was wide, soft, and fat, just the way YB liked it. He went crazy on her from behind as she tried to throw her ass back. She couldn't because his dick was so big and thick, it felt like he was tearing her apart.

"Mmmmm fuck. I – I –can't take I- I- I- t," she belted as her body was rocking the hotel headboard, making loud banging noise.

Blossom came twice before he pulled out. She turned around to see him squirting his semen out, but she rushed to catch it and began sucking his dick. She deep throating his whole dick and lapping up and down as his cum oozed out.

"Damn, you suck a good dick," he said, as she smiled laying down out of breath.

"I had no clue you were packing like that. You almost killed me," she stated as he laid next to her.

"You're from Flatbush, right? he asked.

"Yeah," she responded with her Haitian accent.

"Sleepy got that shit on lock over there."

"Yeah, that's my sorry ass, deadbeat father of my first child. Can you roll up a blunt?" she said as her wig fell off and YB saw she had a low Caesar.

"I hate deadbeat nigga. I'm sorry to hear that, love," YB said rolling up a blunt for her.

"Yeah its cool. He's over there on Church Ave. fucking with my co-worker. That's how grimy he is, but how old are you, daddy? I'm thirty-five, but you look so young," Blossom told him as he past her a rolled blunt in a Dutch master.

"I'm nineteen. I'ma go use the bathroom," he said. Just as he revealed his age, she choked on the blunt. She was the mother to a seventeen-year-old.

YB went in the bathroom and texted Murda, Sleepy's location and got dressed. As soon as he came out the bathroom, Blossom had his gun pointed at him.

"Nigga, you think I'm dumb? I'ma Brooklyn bitch. Who sent you nigga and what do you want with my baby's father? Speak!" she said holding the pistol with two hands, as he laughed.

"I like your style, but I wasn't even going to kill you," he said walking towards her.

"Stop or I'll shoot," she said as he was walking towards her. She pulled the trigger twice, getting nothing except a click

YB punched her in the face, knocking her on the floor and snatching the gun from her.

"You stank pussy bitch. Next time check the clip," he said pulling the clip out of his pocket, loading it inside the glock as she started to cry. YB never kept a loaded pistol around a bitch because he didn't trust them.

YB shot her three times in the head, took her purse and phone, then left the hotel in a rush, hopping in the black Mazda sedan.

***

Flatbush

Murda sat behind the wheel of the black Nissan Maxima, on Church Ave. He didn't know building Sleepy was in, but he did know he was parked three cars behind his sky-blue Audi Q8 truck on rims.

It was close to two in the morning, so the block was pitch black, dirty, quiet and cold.

Murda couldn't sleep for a week after his last encounter with Sleepy. He heard stories of how he killed two of his workers because they didn't want to sell drugs for him no more.

He'd rather make a move first, then get moved on. That was his motto and tonight, he was going to stand on that.

Thirty minutes later, he saw Sleep trembling out of a brick building alone with his car keys in his hand. Murda pulled his hoodie down and grabbed his gun.

Sleepy just left Candy's crib. Candy was a stripper bitch who had some fire pussy and a mean head game. He fell asleep, but he had his own spot on Rutland Road, where he was heading now.

He told his little brother to kill Murda. He didn't know what was taking Trap so long but Sleepy hated to be crossed or feel like he was played.

He was still a little tipsy from the Patron he was drinking with Candy added to the few nutcrackers from London Ave.

Sleepy was opening in his Audi door, when he felt the cold steel to his bald head.

"Take the chain and watch, but you will regret this," Sleepy said, wondering who was dumb enough to rob him in his own hood.

"You can die with that shit and I'm sure it will look good in your casket in your suit," Murda spoke.

"Murda, that's you?" Sleepy said knowing the smooth voice from anywhere. "You're a fucking dead man, nigga. Suck my fat dick you..."

BOOM.

BOOM.

BOOM.

BOOM.

Sleepy's brains flew on the windshield of his Audi.

Murda had blood all over his face as he hopped in his Nissan making a U-turn and rushing off the block, as he heard shots coming in his direction, almost taking out his back window.

Chapter Eight
White Plains Mall
Months Later

Jamika was in the Balmain clothing store on the third floor with her best friend and old college roommate, Robin. The two stayed thick as wool ever since, even though they lived two different lifestyles.

Her friend, Robin, was a beautiful Puerto Rican woman born and raised in the Bronx. At twenty-eight, she was already divorced with a five-year-old son.

Robin worked as a clerk for a city hall in the Bronx. Her life was boring but she went out to party every weekend and she tried her best to bring Jamika along with her so she could get some excitement in her life.

"Girl, this dress would look so good on you. Trust me, you can't hide that big ass under cargo pants all day," Robin told Jamika as she was looking at a tight red strapless gown.

"Robin, you crazy? I'm not wearing no shit like that." Jamika said. Since winter was over, it was time for her to upgrade her wardrobe for Spring.

Lately, work had been great for her. She had been very busy with cases throughout the city because her boss had been trying to crack down on the biggest gangs in New York. Mack Ballers and YGs as well as a section of the Crips that called themselves Dirt Gang, were all on her radar. They were all making a name for themselves throughout Harlem and unfortunately, attracting the police in the process.

"I hope you're ready to hit this club tonight. I been hearing about this spot in the city called the Web Lounge but it's a strict dress code," Robin stated as they walked around the store.

"I believe I heard of it also. Isn't that the place with like two levels or something?" Jamika asked seeing a purse see liked. She checked the tag and saw it was $16,000, which was way too much for her.

"Yeah that it. Oh my God girl, you see that sexy piece of chocolate over there," Robin said as she tapped Jamika's shoulder causing her to look to see what she was hyped up about.

When Jamika saw the man in a nice button up and gray slacks with designer shoes standing by the shoe section, her pussy got moist.

"Damn," Jamika said a little too loud. Seeing his big muscle poking out of his fitted shirt, waves, perfect skin, and clean face, he looked like he had class, and this was her type.

"Jamika. Jamika." Robin snapped her girl out her trace.

"Oh."

"Go say something," Robin suggested.

"Hell no. I don't know that man and I don't even know what to say," Jamika said, not use to approaching men because she was shy. Normally men approached her all day, but she would always decline.

"If you don't walk your ass over there, I will for you," Robin gritted seriously, and Jamika knew how crazy and blunt her friend was.

"Ok, come with me." Robin was pushing Jamika towards the man who was now trying on Balmain shoes.

"Excuse me. I don't mean to interrupt you, but you have a nice taste," Jamika said nervously finding anything to say. The man laughed as he looked at Jamika and her friend. He was caught in Jamika's beauty. Even without make-up, she was still a dime.

"Thank you, but it seems you have good taste as well," Stacks said looking at her Chanel, Gucci and Fendi bags in her hands.

"She sure does. Hey this is Jamika and I'm her friend, Robin. Do you have any friends?" she said cutting straight to the point as he laughed.

"Oh my God! Excuse my friend," Jamika stated.

"It's cool but I'm about to leave if y'all leaving. I wouldn't mind helping you with your bags," Stacks stated checking his Audemars Piguet watch.

"Yeah, we were just leaving," Robin said passing him Jamika's bags as Jamika was blushing.

"Mr. Sanders, did you get the gifts we sent you?" the clerk said as she saw their best customer walking out.

"Yes, thank you," he said before exiting. On the way to the garage area, Robin mainly did all the talking.

Once in the parking lot, he stepped up the a nice, clean new, white, wide body Lexus LS 500 sedan.

"You parked next to me," Stacks said hitting his alarm on his gray Porsche Panamera Turbo with chrome rims.

"Wow, that's a nice car," Jamika stated wondering if he was rich or something. Whatever it was, she liked him.

"Take my number. Hit me when you're free," he said grabbing her phone after placing her bags in her trunk. After he gave her his number, he hopped in the Porsche and pulled out. Jamika felt like she got her groove back and was ready to hit the city nightlife.

***

Web Lounge

Stacks was inside Web's office sitting on his Armani/Casa couch, listening to his boss talk about business as always.

"Yo, Stacks. I'm telling you, son, when this sausage eating motherfucker finds out I'm behind buying all his property he wanted, he's going to be sick," Web said with an evil grin

"He doesn't even know who you are. Mussari never told the mob who he was working for. He just told them a wealthy man." Stacks stated remembered the conversation he had with Mussari before he killed him.

"Well, they gonna find out who I am sooner or later. We run New York. I am buying out every property, lease, or stock that Joe even thinks about putting his hands in. I'll never let no racist cracker John Gotti wannabe run me out of my city," Web said as he banged his fist on his desk.

"Everything's going to fall in place, but when is the next shipment?" Stacks asked, changing the subject because he knew his friend got heated when it came to his legit business.

"I am flying out to Columbia to meet with Rafael in a couple of days," Web said as Stacks stood up. He looked downstairs on the first floor to see people enjoying themselves dancing and drinking but one person caught his eye by the bar.

"Web, I'll see you later," Stacks said, grabbing his white Gucci blazer and headed out of the door.

"You must see some pussy. Go do you, playboy. I gotta shoot out to Las Vegas," Web said locking up his safe filled with millions. He called a private jet to JFK airport. He planned to go out to Vegas to have a couple of threesomes and enjoy himself.

***

Jamika was sitting at the bar drinking a club soda bobbing her head to *Juicy* by Biggie, while Robin was on the dance floor, dancing her ass off.

Jamika wore a black Versace one-shoulder satin dress with Versace six-inch heel, with diamond earrings, a bracelet, a little make-up and her long hair flat ironed straight and hanging down her upper back.

She looked beautiful. Over eight niggas approached her trying to bag her and offered her a drink but she didn't drink or smoke. She kindly denied all their offers, including offers to dance.

"Excuse me. May I join?" a male voice said behind her. She didn't even look back, but she could smell the Dior for men perfume, which smelled amazing

"No thank you. I am gay," she said as she turned around to see Stacks. "Oh my God. Hey. I'm so sorry. I thought you was someone else," she said, feeling embarrassed.

"It's cool. You sure know how to run a nigga away," he laughed." You look stunning tonight," he said as she smiled

"You do too. What are you doing here? Are you following me?" she said over the loud Drake music as he sat in the stool next to her.

"Mr. Sanders, can I help you with anything?" an older white bartender man asked while wiping down the wood grain bar.

"Serve free drinks for the rest of the night. It's on me," Stacks said

"Yes sir," the bartender said looking at his date knowing Stacks had a winner.

"You must be someone very important, Mr. Sanders," she smiled.

"I just know the owner." He took in her neatly polished white and black manicured nails.

"So, what do you do for a living?" Jamika asked the question she been feigning to ask him all day.

"I'm a business owner. I own a lot of stocks and bonds, but I also own a chain of Auto Body shops throughout the city," he said truthfully, as she breathed a sigh of relief. He was legit. "How about yourself?" he said looking at her beautiful flawless skin.

Jamika paused. This was one reason why she was single because when she told people she was a federal agent. They would run away from her.

"I work for the state. A little state job to help pay the bills," she lied.

"Ok, that's what's up," Stacks said. The two enjoyed the rest of the night together and planned to go in a real date soon.

Jamika was very impressed by him. He was everything she wanted in a man. She felt bad about lying to him about her job, but she had to, until the time was right.

Chapter Nine
Bed-Stuy, BK

Murda was sitting in front of Thompkins projects in Bed-Stuy do or die, which was a dangerous violent neighborhood. Murda was posted up on the walkway rail talking to his man, Tails, who was a Gangster Disciple. He had the hood on lock when he wasn't on the Island or up north.

Lately, the Pink Houses were on fire. The police were running in there every day because of the reckless shootings that had been going on. At least four civilians were pronounced dead after the shooting.

Since Sleepy's death his brother, Trap had been on a rampage to kill Murda. Trap knew he was the only one responsible for his brother's death.

Trap was sending his goons in Murda's projects looking for him. They ended up shooting the place up, but Murda's crew was shooting back every time, chasing Trap's men out of their hood.

Murda was also sending hits to Flatbush, killing some of Trap's men. Murda was going tit for tat. Murda was now getting money all over Brooklyn since he was getting keys at a low rate. He would sell them double or for a little lower, but the product was grade A work.

With so much money flowing in, he had to buy a real safe instead of shoeboxes. He also rented a low-key apartment near the Milk River Club, blocks away. Not to mention, he traded his Camaro in for a red Bentley Continental GT with inside adorned with quilted leather polished chrome, flat screen televisions, and five percent tints.

After speaking to Tails about the fifteen keys he had for him, he made his way to Fort Green to holla at another client.

Murda's birthday was coming and he planned to go to Miami and enjoy himself. He didn't care about the little hood beef.

***

Flatbush

Trap was lying in his king size bed next to a thot bitch who lived on his block. Everything was going wrong for Trap since his brother's death. He now had no connect and his brother only had seventeen keys and fifty bands in his stash. It was almost gone.

He had been hearing about Murda riding around Brooklyn in a Bentley GT. This brought fire to his veins. He had been sending niggas to the projects daily to always come up short, but he knew if he didn't push his shit back first, he would end up like his brother.

Trap came up with an idea, but it would take some time to make possible. He knew he had to start right now.

"Yo, bitch. Wake up," he yelled, pushing the young dark-skin, skinny bitch. He was already irritated because she smoked all of his week and had trash pussy. Now she was snoring in his bed as if she put in some work. "Bitch get your shit and get the fuck out. You done smoked up all my shit." Trap kicked out of the bed and onto the wooden floor, in her Pink bra and panties.

"Damn, Trap. It's like that?" she asked. He tossed her clothes to her along with her knock off Coach purse and big ass Air Max 95s.

Once she was out, Trap started to put his plan together once and for all.

***

Manhattan

Freddy was inside of Todd Radziwill's downtown apartment with two of his guards.

"Now, Todd, just so we have a understanding, my boss gave you orders that you didn't follow. To every action, there is a reaction," Freddy said as he walked into his kitchen and came out with a steak knife.

"Freddy, I had no control over that. You know I respect, Joe, but I never made Joe no promises or to Vinny. I'm only co-owner to the markets I sold," Todd said as Freddy's two guards had the man strapped down to one of his dining room chairs.

Todd was a businessowner who sold Joe a couple of his properties in the past, so they always had a good business relationship with each other.

"Who did you sell the establishments to Todd? Your wife and kids will be home soon. Just tell me, so I can be on my way, pal. Business is never personal," Freddy said smoothly, standing in front of him.

Freddy was in his mid-forties, healthy, tall, with slick dark hair short length, handsome, low spoken, and he loved violence. Born in Brooklyn and into the mob, he climbed his way to the top because of his vicious and violent acts he inflicted on other mob families.

"Come on, Fred. I can't discuss." Freddy slammed the steak knife into his right upper thigh, as he screamed in pain.

"Do I have to ask you again?" Freddy said, yanking the knife out his thigh with blood dripping from it.

"Fred, I…I…" Without hesitation, Freddy now forced the knife into Todd's right hand as he screamed, but the two guards covered his mouth.

"Todd, the next one is going to be your little woodpecker," Freddy said in his Italian accen.t

"Ok his name is Web. He is a black man. This motherfucker is crazy. He kidnapped my wife and kids and threatened to kill them if I didn't sell him Joe's properties, I had for him," Todd cried as the knife was still in his hand.

"Was that hard?"

"This guy is different. He is dangerous and rich. Please keep me out of this," Todd said getting lightheaded.

"No worries on that," Freddy said as he shot Todd twice in his heart before walking out.

***

Web was on a private jet G6 sinking in the white leather seats, staring at the stars. He was lost in deep thought. There were five exotic Spanish women slumped everywhere on the jet. They were either high or drunk and Web fucked all of them in a orgy they had two hours ago on the jet.

Now, they were on the way to Colombia, but the women thought they were going to New York.

Web took this trip four times a year, since he and his connect were very close. He made Web a millionaire.

Checking his Rolex. He knew he had forty minutes before the jet landed, so Web screwed the silencer on his Germany Roger pistol and shot all five women in the head so they could never speak on the incident they experienced with him. He then tossed the bodies in the back room. His pilot was on his payroll so he would get rid of the bodies when they landed.

Chapter Ten
Ibague, Colombia

Web was in the back of an all-black SUV being escorted by three other SUV's behind him as he headed to Rafael's mansion.

Web loved the sight of Colombia. Their high Andes Mountains, eastern lowland plains (Llanos), the tropical trees, tropical cool climates, their active volcanoes and the fancy inner-city skyscrapers.

After a half of hour of driving on country farm roads, he started to see the poverty line. Colombia is the largest source of Latin American refugees in Latin America.

The truck drove up a rocky narrow path surrounded by perfect manicured grass. There was so much land, it looked like a golf course.

Once at the high steel bar gate, they entered the large driveway to see a waterfall in the middle and luxury cars parked everywhere.

The mansion was an antique castle, made in the eighteen hundreds with fourteen bedrooms, ten bathrooms, guest house, a large pool area, a beautiful courtyard, and antique Moroccan rugs throughout, filling the 8,912 square feet house.

Guards were surrounding the area with assault rifles in army uniforms, patrolling the compound.

Web was on first name bases with everyone. He greeted everyone as he walked upstairs to see gold Chandeliers hanging from the high ceiling. He stared in admiration as he walked down the hallway.

Once at the French double doors, he knocked twice as he heard someone tell him to come in.

When Web walked in the large library, he saw four large bookshelves with ladders in the sun drenched room, a long Bottega Veneta desk with the matching chairs, vintage mirrors, Bottega Veneta curtains, and decorative painting in the library walls.

"Web, good to see you and you had a safe flight, I see," Rafael said as he closed his reading book and took off his glasses.

Rafael was a very powerful man in his country. He was the leader if the Colombian Cartel and his sister ran the Venezuelan Cartel Family. Their bloodline was built around the cartels for over one hundred years. He only hoped to pass it down to his son.

At sixty-four, Rafael was still active and healthy. He exercised daily by jogging, swimming, and hiking to stay fit. He was five-nine, slim, with a gray goatee and long hair he placed in a ponytail. He was a good-looking man for his age and a smooth talker. His son lived in Bogota, the capital of Colombia and his daughter was a defensive lawyer in the DC.

"Yeah I needed a trip anyway. What's going on?" Web inquired, sitting down taking off his Canali blazer and placing it on his lap.

"I want to start shipping you the drugs in cargo's instead of planes because I hear somehow, the feds are snooping around my aircrafts. My inside helpers can only do so much when they higher power coming into the picture," Rafael stated as Web had a small look of concern on his face.

"So, you think they on to us?" Web asked.

"No, I'm too smart for that. Nothing can never be linked back to us," Rafael told him in his strong Spanish accent.

"The closet safest cargo desk is in New Jersey. I'm sure Stacks has men out there so it would be easy," Web said thinking about it and how it could work.

"Alright good but I want you to meet my daughter, Carmilla. She lives in D.C. If you don't mind, can you fly her back to the states? You two are the same age. Y'all are perfect for each other," Rafael said calling his daughter on the intercom.

Seconds later, the most beautiful woman Web ever saw, walked into the library as they both made a strong eye connection.

"Yes, daddy," Carmilla said trying her best not to look at the handsome man she saw coming into the house.

"This is Web, my good friend. He is going to the states. You can get a lift with him if you'd like," her father stated, trying to play match maker.

"I don't want to be a hassle. I can wait for your jet to come back," she said looking at how perfect Web's facial structure was. It was almost as if he was handmade.

"No please, be my guest. I hate flying alone away."

"You sure?" She replied with her sweet voice.

"Positive."

"Take care of my baby girl," Rafael smiled knowing Web was a good man.

"Daddyyy," Carmilla whined, feeling embarrassed as she left the room in her sunflower Miu Miu satin dress and heels.

Carmilla looked like the model, Rita Ora but better because she had real long blonde hair, thick dick sucking lips, blue eyes, and measurements of 34-26-36. She was thick with a small waist and flat stomach. Her smile was worth a million dollars. She rarely wore make-up because she had natural beauty. At thirty-eight-years-old, she still looked

Romell Tukes

eighteen. That's because she worked out and ate healthy as a vegan.

On the flight back, it was a little quiet at first until Web opened up. Within ten minutes, they both were laughing and having deep conversation. She informed him she lived in D.C., but she had a condo in New York that she visited frequently.

When the flight landed in D.C., they both wished that they could spend more time together, but she promised him next week, she would visit him if she wasn't tied up with criminal cases at her law firm.

The rest of the ride to New York, Web couldn't get her out of his head. She was everything he wanted in a woman.

***

Miami, FL

Murda, YB, Gunna, and eight goons from Brooklyn were in the club Broadway. They were in the VIP section surrounded by twenty bottles of all types of liquor in celebration of Murda's twentieth birthday.

They all rented luxury foreign cars for the weekend so they could stunt in Miami. Last night they had a pool party at the mansion they rented out. It was fucking everywhere, including in the pool, on the roof, and in the driveway. They were all having a good time as Murda paid the way for everybody. Nobody came out their pockets.

"Yo bro. This shit lit," Gunna said sitting next to his brother, drunk out of his mind as he tipped up a bottle of Ace of Spade. Gunna looked like his brother but had brown-skin and stood six foot four. He had the body build of a basketball player for a seventeen-year-old. He wore his curly hair at a low afro with a taped-up fade. The females loved him and

68

they knew he was the future of the NBA. He was the best point guard to come out of Brooklyn in a long time. Everybody knew the kid.

"Glad you're having fun but no more drinking, nigga. You wild saucy," Murda said taking his bottle. He loved his little brother and he always wanted the best for him.

"Damn, son. Let me live," Gunna said with a slur.

"I'ma go grab one of them Cuban bitches on the dance floor nigga," Murda said as Gunna saw a gang of bad Spanish bitches dancing along to a Pitbull song.

"I'll be back," Gunna said, as he left the VIP with a couple of niggas from his hood to hit the dancefloor.

"KD ain't got shit on him but happy birthday, Skrap. We gotta pull up down here more often. Let's hit up Miami Live tomorrow. I heard on Sunday's that shit be lit, son. You heard," YB said as Murda was pouring himself some Dom P.

"Facts. Life is good, homie. Cheers," Murda said to everybody in the section.

The rest of the night was live. Gunna brought back ten Cuban bitches to the VIP, who was looking for the after party at their spot.

***

Brooklyn, NY
Cypress Projects

India was waiting outside in the back of Cypress projects down the street from her house. None of the drug dealers would sell her drugs because they feared they would end up like Real and his brother.

India heard about Real's death. She knew her son was responsible, but she really blamed herself, but she couldn't fight the monkey that was on her back. She been trying for years but her life depended on getting high.

She pulled out her Obama phone and called Smooth again so he could bring out some crack. She had money she stole from Gunna's dresser.

He was in Miami with his brother so she figured she would find a way to replace it before her realized it was gone, or at least that was her plan.

India was shaking. It was a chilly night and her lips were chapped.

"You looking for me?" a voice said from behind her.

"Smooth."

BOOM.

BOOM.

BOOM.

The bullets ripped through her skull and eye socket, as her body fell on the walking rail.

Trap ran off with a smoking gun in an old minivan. He been watching India for two days. He saw her picture of Gunna's Facebook and he found out she was Murda's mom also from the comments. Everybody knew Gunna was Murda's brother in BK.

Chapter Eleven
Ossining, NY
Sing-Sing Prison

Tookie was walking out the gates of one of the best maximum prisons he's been too. All the correctional officers were black. It was going to be a good spot. Most prisons in New York state had big white racist ex NFL built officers jacked up on steroids ready to knock a niggas teeth out.

Tookie was happy to be a free man as he looked behind him at the large cement wall that surrounded the prison that was directly on the edge of the Hudson River.

Looking around, he wondered where the fuck YB was. He told him would be there early. Luckily it was now springtime, so it was a nice breeze.

YB sent him a red Balenciaga sweat suit with a pair of red and black Jordan Retro 11's.

When he saw the new black Cadillac GTSX speeding in front of the prison, he backed up thinking it was a C.O. coming to work because they tended to come in fly ass luxury cars.

"What's popping, you big scary looking nigga?" YB stated as he rolled down the window in front of his big brother who was holding a plastic bag.

"Nigga, you stole this shit? I know you not tripping like that, Skrap," Tookie asked with his screw face not trying come back to jail on his first day.

"Nah nigga. I'm not fucking dumb. This is my shit. Get in so I can update you," YB said blasting Uncle Murda's mixtape until Tookie got in and turned it down.

"Rule number one, never touch a black man's radio." YB pulled off driving down the one-way block, until he got to Spring Street.

"Whatever. Where is Murda? He told me he was coming," Tookie said, admiring the black leather seats, acceleration power, and new car smell. He had no clue his brother was doing it like this. Robbing must've been good. Fresh home, Tookie's mind wasn't on robbing. He was older now with an eight-year-old daughter to raise.

"Murda is laying low since his mom was murdered a couple of weeks ago," YB stated.

"Nah, son. Not India," Tookie said about the lady he had a crush on since he was a little kid.

"Word, son. We been beefing heavy with Trap and them Flatbush niggas and niggas from 90's. You heard," YB said pushing the car down the highway hitting seventy-five miles per hour in a fifty mile per hour zone.

"How the fuck this happened?" Tookie said knowing Trap's little ass real well. The two did two Rikers stunts on the Beacon years ago and he was a live wire, cutting everything moving. He was shaking the building. A lot of niggas feared him, and he beat a couple of bodies years ago so he had a rep as a gun clopper.

"Murda killed Sleepy."

"He what? The plug Sleepy?"

"Yeah now it's lit, but Trap's hiding out. Bro, it's different from when you left. Guess who got Brooklyn on lock now?" YB asked with a devilish smile.

"Who? 'Cause they gotta pay dues."

"Murda."

"Who? Murda? Ain't no way! This nigga was pushing nicks when I was out, son," Tookie laughed, shocked by the news.

"Yo, bro. This nigga supplying Brooklyn. He stunting in a Bentley and all that. Word to the B'z, Skrap. He's up so you know I'm up. I ain't rob a nigga in months," YB said making Tookie laugh.

"He got a gift for you too, but first we about go shopping. You smell like jail, nigga," YB said.

"Whatever, fam," Tookie said turning up the music thinking about what he heard. Murda and Tookie were the big homies in East New York for their Blood gang, but Tookie was focusing on chasing a bag. He left all that extra gangbanging shit behind the wall.

***

BeeHive Lounge

Tookie, YB, and Murda were in the club sixty deep enjoying the night as they bought the bar out for the night.

"I'm sorry to hear about mama love, blood," Tookie said to Murda. Murda was engrossed in his conversation with Erica who was offering a blow job for a nightcap.

"No doubt, my nigga. It's the game but I'm glad you home, bro. I need you on the team. I'm seeing big money and I want you to eat too," Murda said as his Jesus piece and AP watch hit the club lights.

"Say no more, fam. I'm down. You know how we do. I got you," Tookie said.

"I gotta run but here, this is for you. The hotel key is for the Marriott hotel. There are two bitches waiting for you in room 116. Those keys are to the red Audi A7 outside. Welcome home. I love you, bro. Check the trunk," Murda said embracing everybody as he left the club. He wasn't really feeling it after burying his mom two weeks ago.

Murda was on the hunt for Trap. He even had a bounty of one hundred thousand dollars on his location, but the nigga got ghost on him.

When Tookie left the club, he saw the red Audi. He was excited. He never had a luxury car in his life. When he popped the trunk, he saw a Draco with a drum attached to it and two 45's. He also saw a black Fendi bookbag. When he opened it, he saw all blue faces.

"This shit can't be real," Tookie said as he hopped in the Audi to see his crew. His brother and them went to club Lust, but he was on his way to the hotel to see what else Murda had in store for him.

***

Westchester County

"Ummmm. Shit Chelsea," Chris said as his wife was putting on, having him go crazy as she took his dick in and out the back of her warm, moist throat.

They been fucking for an hour and a half. She was just finishing the job

Chelsea was sucking his dick so viciously, it looked like foam was coming out her mouth.

This was one reason why he fell in love with the snow bunny. Her head and pussy was top notch.

Her head was going wild as she slurped his pre-cum while twisting her head on the tip of his dick and jerking his shaft.

"It's cumming," he moaned.

Like clockwork, she caught every drop of the thick semen that spilled out like a waterfall, swallowing everything.

When she was done, she climbed on her side of the bed and brushed her blonde hair back then placed it into a ponytail as she did every night.

Chelsea was beautiful, tall, had blue sparkly eyes, long blonde hair, petite frame, small B-cup breast, perfect teeth, long eyelashes, and sex appeal.

She wasn't your average white chick. Her family was from Italy and was all part of the Mafia. She was raised in Brooklyn with her mother in Coney Island, so she was an official white girl with education and street smarts. She fell in love with Chris in college where she met him and the two have been together ever since.

They had the family, house, cars, white fence, and everything one can ask for but there was one she was always concerned about, which was his gambling habit.

Chelsea was a CNA at the White Plains Hospital and she was a full-time mom to her two children. Normally, Chris was at work or somewhere gambling so spending quality family time wasn't in his daily routine, but he did get the kids ready for school every morning.

"Baby what's wrong? Lately you been acting different," she asked lying naked next to him.

"I'm in debt again, baby."

"What!!! Are you fucking serious? I thought you cleared your tab," she yelled pissed off.

"I did. I did but shit happens baby. I'ma get help."

"You know how many times I heard this?" she said crossing her arms mad at him.

"I am."

"How much do you need this time?"

"One hundred thousand dollars."

"What? Are you serious? Where am I going to get that type of money?"

"A loan and I cover the rest," he said smiling under his sad facial expression

"There's more," said Chelsea.

"Chris, get the fuck out the bed. Go in the guest room. I can't even look at you. Look what you're doing to your family. You know the Mafia doesn't play. I know! They are my fucking family," she screamed as he climbed out the bed knowing she was pissed.

"I'm sorry. I love you," he said as he heard her suck her teeth and tossed a pillow at him on the way out.

Chapter Twelve

"Hey baby," Erica said walking into their polished apartment in her work uniform.

"What's shaking, ma? Come here for a minute," Murda said from the back room.

Lately, shit has been amazing between the couple. They been spending a lot of time together, especially since his mom's death.

"Why your ass ain't text me all day?" Walking into her room, she seen a white small Yorkie dog sitting near her bed.

"Oh my God, baby!" Erica shouted as she grabbed the dog hugging and kissing it.

"I know you always wanted one, but I'm not cleaning his shit," Murda said laughing as he grabbed the Zimmerman box off the table. Opening the gray box, He pulled out a diamond encrusted necklace worth $125,000.

"You out doing yourself today, Papi," Erica said in her Spanish tone as he placed the necklace around her neck.

"Somethin' light, baby."

"Oh yeah? Well, let me go take a shower. You got a bitches pussy wet," she said grabbing his dick ready to fuck

"Hurry up so I can tear that ass up. Lock that dog in the cage in the guest room. Having sex in front of a dog is weird," Murda said as she walked off with the dog.

The lovebirds had crazy rough sex for hours. Erica let him fuck her in every hole, including anal for her second time, but she loved the hard cum from the anal she experienced.

***

Next Day

MDG, Brooklyn

Erica entered the jail. After going through the metal detector, she was brought into a big bright visiting room with long tables, circle round tables, and private booths for legal visits.

This was her second time here to see her brother, Troy. Last time she had to change her clothes twice before she could visit him, so she kept it plain with Gucci jeans and heels with a Gucci blouse.

All eyes were on her as she waited on Troy. She was used to attention, but the way the inmates looked at her, made her feel uncomfortable as if she was a piece of meat.

After twenty minutes of waiting, she saw her brother walk through the door in a brown jumpsuit with a pair of Dolce & Gabbana glasses looking like a GQ model instead of an inmate.

Troy was twenty-four, handsome, tall, slim, tatted up, with thick wavy hair, and colorful eyes He was a Puerto Rican Blood gang member.

Months ago, he was indicted on a twenty-seven-man RICO for drugs, weapons, shootings, and scamming. Troy was at the top of the indictment and Jamika was his arresting officer. That was a big case she got under her belt.

"Sis, what's good?" Troy said hugging her as niggas got a quick peak at her ample round ass.

"Hey, Troy. How are you holding up? Everybody be asking about you," Erica said. She loved her brother despite the fact he was in jail.

"I'm maintaining, you heard? Fighting for my life in here," he said sadly

"What are they talking about?" she asked in Spanish

"Thirty-five to sixty years."

"Troy, you can't be serious," she said, as her eyes got watery

"Yeah, unless I can get them someone in return." He shook his head, not even liking the feeling of being a rat.

"Huh?" she inquired, looking at him oddly because she was a Brooklyn bitch and snitching wasn't in the blood.

"I have to give them someone in position out there, getting big money and this is where I need you at sis," he stated

"You need me for what?" she said shocked

"Murda." Murda's name was ringing in the building. That was the only name Brooklyn niggas mention fresh off the streets and Troy was squeezing informing out of his homies.

"Troy, have you lost your fucking mind? You know how he gets down," she said in Spanish

"Erica, he is my only way out of here. I need you. Please, you're all I have. That nigga is just a piece of dick. From what I hear, he's in clubs, fuckin' all types of bitches. You better go get checked," Troy lied.

"Troy, I love him. I can't. I wouldn't be able to live with myself," she said honestly.

"Well it's me or him. If you come to your senses, call this number. Her name is Jamika. She's an agent. Tell her everything," Troy said handing her a business card with Jamika's number on it. Troy got up and left leaving her pretty face in tears.

***

Manhattan, NY

Stacks and Jamika were officially on their first date at Mr. Chow's, which was a classy, Hibachi restaurant downtown.

"I must say I'm impressed you know how to cater," Jamika stated eating her food. She wore a Satin Chanel purple dress with the pumps to match.

"I try, but I'm glad to finally get to spend some time with you. The little texting, we do isn't really enough when you be on my mind all day!" Stacks stated as he loosened the tie on his blue, Ralph Lauren suit.

"I be so busy. I'm sorry, but I've been thinking about you as well and spending more time with you is something I look forward to," she stated honestly.

Jamika recently did a background check on Stacks and he was everything he said he was. He was a successful business owner with no felons. She felt like she hit the lottery.

"Good, now how was it for you growing up?" Stacks asked. Jamika gave him the run down on her life leaving out certain things, but she was honest. They enjoyed their night and then went for a walk in Central Park, while holding hands.

Chapter Thirteen
Court St, BK

Freddy was in Joe's office with Stacey Adams shoes on Joe's leg rest, blowing cigar smoke out his mouth as Joe was on the phone discussing business.

Most of Joe's businesses were on Court Street in the downtown area of Brooklyn. The area was mostly Italians, all under Joe command.

This was Freddy's first-time seeing Joe in a few weeks because Joe was out in Vegas with other big-name mob families, taking care of business and attending the annual Mafia meeting with families from all over the states.

"Dumb muthafucker." Joe slammed the phone as Freddy laughed because he knew his boss had a nasty, foul mouth for his age.

"What the fuck is so God damn funny, Fred? Where is my money? I haven't seen you in weeks. The fucking gathering was a fucking disgrace, I tell you," Joe complained as always.

"Sorry to hear that, but I gave the money to Miley, as you asked," Joe said.

"Good. I'll never see that again. My daughter has a problem spending money and a lot of money. That's why she is in New Jersey with her mother. I'm blessed all of my other kids have their own shit and none of them give an old man shit, them fucking scumbags."

"Next time step you pull out game up."

"Funny."

"Nah, Joe but for real we have a big issue. When you left, I went to pay Todd a warm visit and he told me some disturbing news. A man by the name of Web has been the one purchasing all of your ideal businesses. Todd said he is very wealthy," Freddy said as his face turn beet red.

"You're telling me a Jew, European, or a Nazi wanna be been playing games with me?" Joe asked not caring for any other nationality expect his own Italian bloodline.

"No, no, that's not the crazy part. Web is black." Freddy watched Joe toss his work phone at his wall, shattering it.

"A fucking NIGGER?" Joe yelled. He was so loud, the whole store heard him including the customers at front.

"Joe it's going to be handled, but I'm hearing he is dangerous, so let me do my research on this guy," Freddy stated.

"Fred, you find out who this cocksucker is and bring me his fucking head attached to his balls," Joe said as Freddy stood to leave because he had to go meet Chris for his payment.

**

Chris was waiting under the Brooklyn Bridge for Freddy to arrive to pay him the $100,000 he had his wife obtain from a bank loan.

Lately, he been busy at work with his partner, Jamika taking on mostly gang cases and R.I.C.O cases throughout the city. He hadn't been able to steal no extra cash or drugs lately. His boss had been on his back because for the past couple of months, a lot of money been coming up missing from the storage in the basement.

When Chris saw the two all black Lincoln Navigators pull up, he grabbed the big brown envelope full of fresh crispy hundreds.

He was parked right next to the water under the bridge where he used to come as a kid to get away from his mother and money hungry brother. After their mom passed of heart failure, Chris and Web had a falling out. The reason was because Web could've paid $200,000.00 to buy her a new heart as the hospital offered but he refused.

Chris knew his brother had the money, but he never understood why he refused to save their mother.

Freddy got out the truck with six goons behind him, thinking he had to toss Chris in the river if he ain't have his $150,000.

"Freddy, man what's up? I'm sorry for the wait," Chris said rushing to hand him the money. He didn't miss the evil crazy vicious look on his face.

"Oh, it must be Christmas again. Which bank did you rob? I know you ain't get no loan, you got bad credit and you're a nigger," Freddy said counting the money while his soldiers laughed along with him.

Chris was used to the racist jokes. It never bothered him because he knew all of their pretty wives wanted some black dick. If the time ever approached, he was going to fuck every white bitch in the MOB family.

"I'ma try to have the rest for you soon," Chris said.

"Ok come back down to the shop. Tell Chelsea I said hi and thank you Let her know to continue them yoga classes too," Freddy laughed as he walked off leaving Chris pissed. He hated when he mentioned Chelsea because he heard he always had a thing for her but Chelsea only dealt with black guys.

Chris was on his way back to work then he was going to go home to fuck the shit out of Chelsea, just because he could

***

Coney Island, BK

Web was walking around the Coney Island theme park with Carmilla having a good time on rides, slot machines, and prize games.

When they got to the boardwalk away from the packed crowds, they sat down to look at the stars and nightfall as the spring breeze started to kick in.

"Today was so fun. Thank you," Carmilla said smiling sitting close to him on a metal bench.

"It was your idea. I had plans for a five-star restaurant and a ride on a yacht on the ocean." He stared at her thick thighs in her Celine jeans.

Web wore a regular Givenchy top and bottom with a pair of sneakers. He kept it very casual today too. He wasn't all about suit and ties, he could switch his swag.

When she told him, she was coming to New York, he was excited. He hadn't stopped thinking about her since he first laid eyes on her.

"I'm a very easy-going girl, Web. I'm not your average woman. I was raised around a dangerous lifestyle. I've seen a lot of bad things and I saw a lot of good, but it made me who I am today. I love to help people, especially criminals because we all do wrong, make mistakes, and live secret lives but there are always two sides to a story in everyone's situation," she stated as Web nodded his head

"Growing up in Brooklyn, it's rough. Niggas are dying everyday over nothing. Little kids are selling drugs to eat dinner at night, kids ten years are missing school because their parents are too high to register them in school. Everything I saw growing up, made me want more and better as well as helping others," Web stated.

"That's why I like you."

"Why?"

"Because I see so much of me in you," she smiled.

84

"I like you too. I never felt so strong about a woman as I do with you," he stated.

"So, why don't you make me yours?" she asked seriously.

"Are you sure? If you're mine, you become a part of me and my life and my life isn't all peaches and cream," he said honestly.

"I was raised in a cartel. I'm pretty sure I can it," she said as he kissed her soft lips.

The two spend the rest of the night boo'd up and happier than ever.

Romell Tukes

Chapter Fourteen
Fishkill, NY

YB and Murda both sat behind the all black Chevrolet Traverse, watching the sky-blue two-story house at the end of the quiet block.

It was 11:30pm and all the lights in the house had just gone off.

"You ready for this?" YB asked Murda as he looked down the dark, middle class neighborhood streets to see if the coast was clear.

"Yeah, but I don't want no mistakes, and nobody is to be left alive in there," Murda stated coldly.

"That's my type of party", YB said pulling his ski mask down on his face as Murda did the same before they got out of the car. They headed towards the back of the house of Sleepy and Trap's mother.

Sleepy moved his mom and little sister upstate years ago to get her out of Flatbush because they were getting money and they knew how Brooklyn niggas were. They would run up in your crib for pennies.

Once they broke through the back door, they stuck to their plan to spilt up as they crept through the kitchen.

Murda saw Jamaican flags everywhere and pictures of Jamaican's in Jamaica on beaches. There was a city of Kingston sign with a couple of dread heads post up around it.

The house was dark but both men were able to maneuver through it as if they had night vision.

Murda climbed up the flight of stairs to see a room to his left. He entered it slowly and saw a fat lady with short dreads snoring so loud, the walls vibrated. He knew it was Trap's mom.

With a silencer already attached to his pistol, he placed it at her head and shot her in the head sixteen times leaving brain noodles on her pillow.

YB was down the hall standing outside of the bedroom door peeping through the door crack. YB's dick was hard while watching Trap's nineteen-year-old little sister play in her fat pussy with a big black dildo.

Trap's sister was a dark skin pretty Jamaican chick with thick long dreads, skinny, big juicy breast and piercings.

YB was looking at her fat pussy taking the whole thirteen inches as her long pussy lips flopped on the side of her extra pussy skin.

"Mmmmm," she moaned with her head leaned back shoving the vibrator in and out her wetness.

YB felt cum dripping down his leg. He couldn't watch no more as he busted inside the room with his gun drawn, causing her to scream as cum poured out of her pussy nonstop. YB shot her in her heart six times then placed two in her head for good measures.

Murda and YB ran downstairs and left the same way they came inside, unnoticed and quiet.

"What took you so long?" Murda asked as he slowly pulled the truck off the curb.

"Nothing, why you ask that?"

"Nigga, you better not be on no freak shit, son! We don't get down like that," Murda said as YB looked offended.

"I have never had to take no pussy. Who do I look like, Bill Cosby, Skrap?" YB inquired a little upset that his friend would disrespect his gangsta like that.

"Just checking," Murda stated as YB was itching his inner thigh.

***

Month Later

Jamika and Stacks had just come from the BB King restaurant downtown. Lately, things been heating up between the two. They been spending a lot of time together, sleeping at each other houses and still controlled their sexual lust.

They were on their way to Jamika's crib. Tonight, the lust was in the air. The two had been grinding and rubbing on each other all night.

Jamika wore a tight Fendi dress and Stacks wore a Versace top and bottom outfit.

Once at Jamika's crib, Stacks parked his Porsche next to her Lexus and followed her upstairs into her apartment.

"You look beautiful tonight, baby," he said looking into her soft eyes as they entered her nice two-bedroom apartment. Her crib was neat and clean with shiny wood floors, photos of black icons, a huge fifty-two inch flat screen hanging on her living room wall.. Jamika had white leather couches throughout the living room and dining room area.

"I'm ready to give myself to you, but you have to treat me right," Jamika said as they both walked to her bedroom.

"I will," Stacks said holding her hand as she got him on her Jimmy Choo sheets. She began taking off her clothes in front of him as he did the same.

Within seconds, the two were kissing and licking each other. Stacks placed the tip of his large dick at the entrance of her small, swollen pussy.

Stacks slowly plunged his dick in and out of her trying to open her tight, wet, warm, pussy as she moaned biting down his glossy lips.

"Mmmmm. Yesss," she cried as Stacks fondled her small breast while kissing her. She gave out a long groan as he pushed his hips deep into her as her hips, pushing upwards, feeling his dick inside of her.

"You like this big dick?"

"Yesss," she screamed as he started pounding her little fat, bald pussy.

Jamika wrapped her legs over his waist as she felt herself about to climax. She clutched her pussy walls.

"Damn," he said feeling her tight pussy walls grip his dick almost making him bust a load in her.

"I'm cummingg-g-g," she said as she came hard. Cum poured out her pussy on to his dick and down her ass, soaking her bed.

Stacks turned her sideway and entered her pumping his dick in and out of her until he got a rhythm. He then slapped her ass cheeks making it jiggle.

"Ugghhhhh. Fuck," she screamed feeling his dick in her lower back, hitting her walls and G-spot.

"You want me?" he gritted going a little deeper as she felt his pelvis diving into her ass while he spread her ass cheeks.

"I'm cumming," she yelled climaxing on his dick as he came with her, pulling out and releasing his load on her back. He then began sucking her pussy from behind

"Ohhh shit," she shouted as he started eating her juicy box from behind.

Stacks moved his tongue viciously in her bare pussy as her body tightened. She cocked one leg in the air as he sucked the cum out her pussy.

"Awwwww. Mmmmmm," Jamika yelled as her legs got numb as she climaxed on him again. She never knew she could cum this hard.

Stacks then bent her over and fucked her doggy style until they both came and went to sleep with a newfound respect for each other.

Romell Tukes

Chapter Fifteen
Brooklyn, NY

Freddy was having a sit down with another mob family at an Italian restaurant on Atlantic Ave.

Gambino was another local mob family from the Williamsburg section of Brooklyn where they controlled the drug game as well as extorted the Jewish owned businessmen.

"Freddy, I'm not one to cut corners or leave you in the blind. I've been buying drugs from you over twenty years but never have I saw much of a decrease in my drug market," Gambino stated taking a deep breath with his fat sloppy three hundred pound frame.

"I'm not fully understanding you, Gambino," Freddy stated looking at the man's beady eyes.

"There is a reason why I'm not seeing no drug profit, Fred. A black fucker named Stacks is taking over all of my areas. His drugs are better and cheaper, Fred. All of my clients are running to his people," Gambino stated sadly.

"This isn't the fucking first time I'm hearing this name. No wonder why I've been seeing a decrease in my turfs lately, Gambino. All my client informed me about this guy. Do you have anything on him?" Freddy asked angrily looking around the empty restaurant.

"No just a name."

"Do me a favor, get anything and everything you can get on this nigger. I got a feeling Brooklyn is about to go back to the 1960's. Get ready for a war, Gambino" a pissed off Freddy stated before leaving.

***

Weeks Later

Trap had just got back from Atlanta where he was lying low after killing Murda's mother. That didn't last long because he caught wind that his mother and sister were killed.

When Trap's aunty told him about this last month, all he could do was cry for days. He was stuck in Atlanta. A tornado hit the city, closing the airport.

His mother had a closed casket funeral because chunks of her head were missing, and it was unrepairable.

He was in New York for one mission only and that was to kill everything Murda loved. Tonight was going to be some healing as he waited in the navy-blue Mustang Shelby GT350.

Trap was parked in a high school parking lot full of cars waiting on Gunna to come out from his big game.

The whole Brooklyn knew who Gunna was because he was the most promising kid to go to the NBA. He killed every basketball tournament in the city scoring over thirty-eight points a game.

Since he couldn't find Murda, he was hunting the next best thing his closet kin.

***

Gunna just got done putting up thirty-four points at a big high school basketball game. Every time he played, he dunked, crossed niggas up, and make 87% of his shots.

"Yo, Gunna what you doing this weekend? I'm trying to hook up," a cute red bone chick from school asked.

Gunna was walking out of the gym in the middle of the large crowd, trying to exit the school since the night game was over.

"Shay, I'm a little busy this weekend but put your number in my phone, and I'ma hit you," he said handing her his phone.

"Aight," she said smiling. She heard rumors about his dick game being on point.

Since Gunna's mother died, he had been staying in Red Hook in a nice one-bedroom apartment Murda paid for. Normally, his girlfriend Faith stayed there. Faith was a beautiful Spanish chick from the Bronx who was raised in Bed-Stuy but she was a full-time college student who was deeply in love with her boo.

Murda also bought him a Jaguar XE to get around in and he loved it. Bitches been on his body since he had been pulling up in the Jag.

"Yo, Gunna, that was a good game, son," one of his teammates stated walking through the parking lot with him.

"Facts, bro. You put up sixteen. That's lit," Gunna said. Suddenly, a weird feeling swept over him. Something in the pit of his stomach let him know that something was wrong.

Bloc.

Bloc.

Bloc.

Bloc.

Bloc.

Everybody started to run and take cover as bullets started flying everywhere. They only lasted for about thirty seconds but felt like forever.

Trap hopped in his Mustang, hitting the gas out the parking, hitting an old woman and her nephew in the process, killing him instantly.

By the time the EMS workers and police arrived, there were four dead body. Shay, the elder woman's nephew and two basketball players were caught in the crossfire.

Luckily, by the time medical arrived at the scene, Gunna was still breathing after being shot five times. He took three in the legs and two in the back.

＊

"What happened? Are you sure it was Gunna?" Murda woke out his sleep turning on the lamp, waking Erica up in the process. "Slow down. Okay I'm on my way," Murda said as he hopped out his bed and started to get dress fast as lightening.

"Baby, what's wrong?" Erica asked as she saw him grab his pistol and car keys.

"Someone shot Gunna."

"Oh shit! You want me to come with you?"

"Nah you safe here. I gotta see what's going on," he said, grabbing his phone rushing out the house.

When Erica heard the door slam, she got of her bed naked and put on her off-white rope. She went through her purse looking for her phone so she could get on social media and send her blessings to Gunna's Instagram page.

Erica and Gunna was Instagram famous with over one million followers and over ten thousand comments daily.

As she was digging through her Bottega Veneta purse, she saw a business card with Jamika's name and number.

Erica started to think about her brother as she had been doing the last couple of weeks.

Tonight, she had to come up with a decision. She loved Murda but she hated the life he lived. She knew he would sometimes step out to cheat on her, which crushed her.

Then it was her brother who raised her and took care of her since she was a kid. She knew he needed her. She was his only option.

Minutes of staring at the card, she made up her mind

Erica texted Jamika's number requesting a time and date to meet somewhere in the city, where they could talk in private.

After sending the text, she knew her life was about to change. She couldn't turn on her blood, but she knew this could damage their relationship for life. She cried herself to sleep that night knowing there was no turning back.

Romell Tukes

Chapter Sixteen
Atlantic City, New Jersey

Chris was in Atlantic City at the blackjack table, watching the dealer's hands for any funny business.

"Hit me," Chris said as he took a sip of Rum and Coke on ice, sweating because he already lost the money he got from Freddy, who was a loan shark as well.

He'd thought he could come to AC and hit up a couple of casinos for a come up.

Chris had been in the casino for six hours and only lost money except when he played the five dollars on a slot machine. He told Chelsea earlier he would be working all night, but little did she know, he took a vacation.

"Twenty, sir. I'm sorry, you missed by one point. Another hand?" the card dealer said snatching his poker chips, as Chris wanted to punch the man in his face, take his chips and run out the casino.

"I'll be right back," Chris said rushing upstairs to his hotel room to get the $25,000 he was saving in case of emergency such as this one.

Chris ran downstairs and traded in every cent for poker chips and he made his way back to the poker table, where lost $70,000 at earlier.

After two hours of gambling, Chris lost all $25,000 and his Rolex watch on a side bet. He knew Chelsea was going to be pissed because she had given him that watch as a birthday gift two years ago.

With the $50,000 he already owed the MOB and now with this $150,000, he was in debt big time. He had no clue what he was going to do as he went upstairs to ponder and stress.

***

Sotto, New York

Jamika was sitting inside of Barnes & Noble bookstore reading an urban novel called *Life of a Savage* from Lockdown Publication while drinking a cup of tea.

The other day when she got the text from Troy's sister informing her, she had to speak to her about something important, she only hoped it was worth her time.

Lately she been very busy with big cases. A lot of blue-collar friends and gang cases throughout the city.

Her and Stacks were officially an item, especially after they had sex for the first time. Now it was an everyday thing. That's one reason why she been in good spirits lately.

Jamika saw a pretty young Spanish chick approaching her in a pair of black Gucci pants and sweater in eighty-five degree with a pair of dark shades.

"Hey I'm Erica, Troy's sister. Thank you for coming out," Erica said placing her purse on the floor while looking around.

"No problem. Thanks for calling." Jamika could clearly see that Erica was nervous. "You ok?" Jamika asked, sensing the girl was really bothered.

"Whatever I tell you must be between us and I don't want my name in the mix. Please, these dudes are dangerous," Erica said catching Jamika's full attention now.

"Ok sure. Of course. That's no problem," Jamika replied pulling out her yellow writing pad and ink pen.

"Will this information help get Troy out? He is the only reason why I'm doing this."

"To be honest Erica, it all depends on how strong this case is," Jamika stated sipping some tea.

"His name is Murda. He is from Pink Houses. He runs a huge drug operation throughout Brooklyn, and he's committed a lot of murders since I've known him. I personal can tell you about six murders I've heard of," Erica stated sharply.

"Heard of or do you know for a fact? Will you be able to stand on it at trial?" Jamika replied.

"I know trust me. You remember them to cops that were murdered in the Pink Houses?"

"Yes. Of course," Jamika said knowing the story really well because the unsolved case was sent to the FBI.

"Well he did it. I overheard him and his best friend YB talking about it."

"How do you know this Murda character?" Jamika asked wondering.

"He's my boyfriend whom I've been with forever. I know everything about him." Erica felt guilty for what she was doing to Murda.

"Can I ask you why?"

"I love my brother and I want to help," Erica said writing shit down.

Jamika knew it was a cold game, but this was as cold as it gets. She couldn't picture telling on a boyfriend she loved. She believed in loyalty and honor.

Erica sat there with Jamika for two hours giving her a full notepad of information on Murda to help her get Troy out of jail. Jamika promised she would do her best to help get him a lesser sentence or no jail time at all.

***

Months Later

It was July 4th and Web and Carmilla were out enjoying the fireworks in downtown Brooklyn.

Business had been good for Web. Everything was falling in place with his new restaurant and new shoe store he just opened.

Web and Rafael been moving tons of coke through the New Jersey parts. Everything was smooth sailing.

Things with Carmilla was heating up. The two couldn't get enough of each other but sex was off limits for Carmilla until marriage.

Carmilla wasn't a virgin but she chose a long time ago to give her hand in marriage before she would give herself to another man.

Tonight, they were at a park near the Barclay's Center watching the fireworks on the riverfront.

"This is so beautiful. I'm glad I've been spending a lot of time with you, Web. When I met you six months ago, I never thought you would be the one who snatch my soul and I damn sure didn't think I would fall in love with you," Carmilla said in her thick Spanish accent while hugging Web from behind.

"I feel the same. Since you came in my life, you're all I could think about. I need you. There is no way around it," Web said turning her around and getting on one knee.

"What are you doing crazy?"

"Carmilla will you marry me?"

"Oh my God! Are you serious?" she asked him with tears in her eyes while covering her mouth.

"Yes baby. I love you," he said being honest, opening the ring box.

"Yesss, I'll marry you," she said jumping up and down in her heels as he placed the $1.7 million diamond ring her finger. That was huge like a rock.

They kissed and enjoyed the rest of the night as Web's security played the background in a GMC truck in the lot.

Lately, he had been traveling with security. It was something he never did but had a feeling that things were about to get extremely hot in the summertime.

Romell Tukes

Chapter Seventeen
Downtown, Brooklyn

"Take your time, bro. One step at a time, son," Murda said as he watched his brother Gunna walk around his living room area with a walker back and forth to regain some strength in his quadricep area.

The night Gunna was shot at his high school basketball game, the doctor told him he would never be able to walk again.

Trap shot out his Articular Capsule (AC) Pes anserinus and his inner thigh pectineus, ending his basketball career.

That was only the half. The bullets that entered his erector spine caused damaged to cervical, thoracic, and lumbar regions, which effects his flexion, bending, and any movement.

Gunna was happy to be alive unlike some of his friends. He saw a lot of killings his whole life. He was from the worst PJ's in Brooklyn, but he never came close to losing his life as he did months ago.

"I'm sick of this shit," Gunna said slowly sitting down.

"Be grateful you walking and alive," Murda responded, getting up to turn off the oven where he was re-warming up some pizza from last night.

"Yeah that's a fact but I've been meaning to speak to you." Gunna lifted his casted foot up placing it on the leg rest in his brother's living room.

"What's up and no I'm not bringing you no weed. You heard what the doctor said, crackhead," Murda said bringing his brother plate of Savage pizza with cheesy crust.

"Thanks, but it's not the weed shit, bro. I don't want to finish school," Gunna said as Murda looked at him as if he was on crazy meds.

"What the fuck you mean? Listen, niggas get shot every day. Shit happens. You bugging the fuck out," Murda yelled.

"You don't know how the fuck this shit feel. I just lost mommy and now I can't even fucking walk. My NBA life is done. That was all I had. Everything I had was snatched from me in months and I wonder whose fault it is," Gunna said as Murda put his head down, because his brother was speaking the truth.

"Look, Gunna. I'm sorry. I never thought shit will get to this level, but I swear I will kill this nigga ten times. I just always had big dreams for you. Since kids, I never wanted but the best for you."

"I understand that but understand that I'm not a kid no more. I'm almost eighteen," Gunna stated.

"You right but if you think dropping out of school is good for you, then I support you but just think about your future is all I'm saying, B. You heard," Murda said checking his AP watch realizing it was time to go meet Tookie.

"Aight, bro. I love you," Gunna said putting the flat screen TV on SportsCenter.

"You got a funny way of showing it, but Erica will be home from work soon to help you. Don't be eye balling my bitches ass, either," Murda joked.

"Shit I'd rather stab my own eyes out."

***

Tompkins Projects

"Hooo…what's popping, Skrap?" Tookie greeted Murda as he embraced him, throwing up the blood set

106

The park was dark and empty. Tookie's baby's mother, Crystal, lived upstairs so this was like his second home, and now thanks to Murda, he was the plug.

Since Tookie been home, his life changed overnight. He was taking care of his family and being able to push an Audi. He got his own crew, money was flowing and he didn't have to rob a nigga to get it.

Tookie had workers so he rarely touched drugs. His workers would pick up the bricks and bust them down.

"What's popping with you, son? Niggas told me you be out here doing pull-ups, dips, and push-ups every morning," Murda said hanging from the monkey bars.

"You know how I do these bitches loving all this big brolicky shit," Tookie laughed.

"What's the status, son?" Murda asked knowing this was the reason why Tookie called him out here.

Murda told Tookie to hunt Trap down and use his connections because everybody knew Tookie was connected throughout New York.

"I got word from my man Black in Mount Vernon saying Trap was out there with some Crip bitch, but he be laying low. I was up top with Black in Greene. He's from seven and third projects. Son's official, you heard," Tookie said seeing fiends walk through the projects.

"Good, keep an eye on him. Play him close. His time is coming but I should re-up sometime this week."

"Aight just hit me, fam. You speak to my brother?" Tookie asked.

"Nah. Last time I checked, he was in Staten Island fucking with Ed and Dex. This nigga selling pounds of weed?" Murda said surprised.

"He what?" Tookie said shocked never knowing YB to sell any drug, only robbing niggas.

"Yeah, son. That shit fucked me up, but I wondered how he got all that weed. I heard it's like fifteen hundred pounds or some crazy number like that," Murda said.

"I think we both know how he got it but I'ma go to Brownsville and the Crown Heights to holler at Day Day and Green eyes. Them niggas are making big moves with me," Tookie said walking out the parking lot, trying not to get his Balenciaga's shoes dirty.

"Hit me," Murda said going the opposite way.

*****

Lil Italy, NY

Joe and Freddy were sitting in the back section of Joe's restaurant eating pasta as other Italian families enjoyed their meals.

"So this nigger thinks he going to open a club in my neighborhood?" Joe laughed after hearing from Freddy that one of the spots Web recently out bid him for, would be a club are lounge/bar.

"That's the talk around the area," Freddy said not really caring for Joe's legit business. He was worried about this Stacks character that was making life rough.

"How's everything coming along with your affairs, Fred?"

"I'm about to try to have a sit down with this Stacks guy. I got a lead on him," Freddy said referring to a friend of a friend who informed him Stacks owned a car shop on Bushwick Ave., only a block away from where Fred grew up at.

"Smart, if something could be talked out then, why not? There is money for everyone, even the black roaches, but they have to fall in line and work under us. They can never be neck to neck with us, Fred. They hate us just as we hate them," Joe stated.

"I know boss, but I have to go. I'll call you later," Freddy said looking at Joe's six security guards posted by the exit door in black suits.

"Ok, I heard your daughter in town."

"Yeah she brought my grandson up. I'ma go spend some time with them," Freddy said leaving as Joe was finishing his meal, thinking how to shut down Web's club plan. Joe was highly upset. He knew nothing about the mystery man that made him even madder.

Chapter Eighteen
Bronx

YB was in posted in the Q Lounge on Gun Hill Road in the Uptown section of the Bronx with Mell and OD.

The place was packed tonight with models and bottle girls serving drinks around the bar and dance floor area where women were dancing to a reggae song.

YB and Mell were playing pool for $3,000 a game and he was up two games, so he felt good as he talked shit.

"All that money you are seeing, nigga we should've bet $5,000 a game, duke," YB said as Mell's long dreads hung on the table as he just missed the corner pocket.

"Nigga, shut up and put your money where your mouth is," Mell said as YB's face turned sour. He didn't like when niggas got smart with their mouth.

"How about you watch your fucking mouth and rack them balls, again? Make sure you pay me my money before I tell you to suck my dick," YB said in a serious tone while taking a sip of Henny from a glass cup.

Mel looked at his best friend, OD, who was good friends with YB. Mel only came out to chill with OD because he heard of YB and his name was like Chucky in the hood. He heard a lot of vicious stories about him.

"I'm good. You won this nine grand right here," Mel said with a Jamaican accent pulling out two big wads of money. Mel sold pills and lean in Tilden projects in Brooklyn. He was considered hood rich.

"That's what I thought," YB said as he snatched the money smiling. He wanted to rob Mel for his chain he had, just because he knew he was a pussy but off the strength of OD, he wouldn't.

"Yo I'm ready to bounce, son," OD said as he threw the pool stick on the table and ice grilled a couple of Bronx niggas. He then walked out because he had a thot in Summer PJ's waiting on him.

YB hated Bronx niggas. He was always told Bronx niggas was on some pretty boy shit and always wanted to be like Brooklyn niggas.

They walked out the side door of the lounge and into the parking lot.

"Yo, YB where... "

Bloc.

Bloc.

Bloc.

Bloc.

Bullets ripped through OD's chest, dropping him as Mel ran and YB pulled out his glock 27 and started shooting back.

Trap was near the fence on the side of a Benz truck trying to take YB's head off.

"You bitch ass niggas. I'ma do you just like I did your sister," YB shouted running from car to car trying to get a good aim at Trap as he saw him a little.

BOOM.

BOOM.

BOOM.

BOOM.

YB was shooting up the Benz truck, hoping to catch him with a wild shot.

Bloc.

Bloc.

Bloc.

Bloc.

Police sirens could be heard because the 47th Street precinct was down the block, so both men hopped in their cars, burning rubbing out of both entrance ways trying to avoid going to jail but mad they miss their shot.

***

Freddy pulled up to Stacks' auto body shop in two white GMC SUV trucks, filled with goons in suits.

Stacks just came from telling VP a new shipment will be tomorrow night.

Walking out the shop garage into the small lot full of broken cars, he saw two white trucks with tints parked next to his Porsche.

At first Stacks thought it was the feds or someone famous needing some car work.

When he saw an older white man climb out in a gray suit with a cigar in his mouth and a couple of big overweight white boys with them, he had a clue it was about to get ugly. Luckily, he was strapped.

"Excuse me. Are you Stacks?" Freddy asked him looking at Stacks' expensive Dior for men suit, not use to seeing black men dress like this.

"That's me. Who are you?" Stacks asked holding his ground, now leaning against his Porsche.

"I don't mean to come to your place of business, but it seems to me that lately you been selling drugs around some of my areas and I don't like to bump heads so I came up with an agreement," Freddy said smiling as if he was friendly.

"And what may that be. Mr..."

"Just call me Fred please, but you can purchase your weight from me and I'll give you Nostrand Ave. and Empire Ave. Everything else is off limits as for as this area, downtown, and Court St," Freddy stated as if this was a hell of a deal.

"Fred, first off I'm a businessman, not a dummy so how about you take your agreement and shove it up your white, hairy ass. I take orders from nobody I'ma self-made man, as you see," Stacks said spreading his arm looking around his car lot.

"So, you want to play hard huh, kid? Are you sure?"

"I'm positive. Maybe you can try your hand on a fresh-man in the game, but definitely not a vet," Stacks replied.

"I don't think you understand what you're doing Stacks," Freddy said as a minor threat. Stacks got off the Porsche and Fred's goons stepped up ready to crush Stacks if he even moved the wrong muscle.

"I don't think you want to threaten a person like me. I'm Freddy Vittario Veneto." Stacks stated smiling, letting the men know he was not as slow as they thought.

"Have it your way. You people are very hardheaded," Freddy said walking off pissed followed by his men.

Stacks did his research on every big drug dealer, espe-cially when he chose to move into their turf to sell drug. He did it just in case something went wrong, just like it just did seconds ago.

Stacks hopped in his Porsche pissed off. He knew Fred was up to something. Now he would be paying close attention to the men.

What Freddy or none of his goon's saw was when VP placed a GSP tracker under Freddy's GMC truck. This was why he kept him on his team because he was always two steps ahead of the game.

***

Lil Italy, NYC

Web just cut the rope for the grand opening of the Central Lounge, dead in the middle of the Mafia turf.

The grand opening was big. It was mainly white people fresh off of work who was there to enjoy the free drinks. The opening was successful with over five hundred people attending in less to two hours.

Web's office was in the back. He was drinking Dom P, watching the cameras as people enjoyed the music. Web had a business partner who was a wealthy Jewish man from Williamsburg, but Web's name was on everything.

He knew this was the beginning to a lot of hate, envy, and jealousy with the MOB, but he was ready for whatever.

The place had eight big, white security guards, a big dance floor, bar, picture booth, restaurant inside, and a large DJ booth for the best DJs in the Tri-State area.

Romell Tukes

Chapter Nineteen
Mount Vernon, NY

"This is it, blood," YB said smiling as him and Murda was looking at the tall, brick project building across the street from a park and playground, full of niggas at midnight.

Murda found out Trap was hiding out in apartment 7a and before he let Trap kill anyone else he loved, he was going to take him out.

"You got your silencer? You know we in the projects," Murda said looking around the dark parking lot area.

"That's a fact, brody. This nigga almost caught me slipping. I got something for his ass," YB smirked.

"Aight, just come on. Put your hoodie on. I don't trust these niggas out here", said Murda.

"Nah, the goonies run this area. Them little niggas official," YB said putting his hoodie over his head.

They both hopped out of the gray Volkswagen Arteon with Timbs on dressed in black sweat suits.

***

Trap was sitting on the living room couch as FeFe was letting him face fuck her as she started to suck faster.

"Uhhmmm…" Trap moaned as he watched her blonde hair dive up and down in his lap.

She had her thick, wet lips locked around his dick, holding on for dear life as he drove his cock down her young throat.

"You love that? The way I suck this dick? I want you to cum in my mouth," she said while playing with the head of his dick with her tongue ring.

PSST.
PSST.
PSST.
Murda shot FeFe in the neck as YB rushed Trap and started to pistol whip him.

"You remember me nigga?"

Whack!
Whack!
Whack!

"Huh bitch nigga?"

Whack!

Blood was squirting everywhere as Trap couldn't even move but he was still breathing.

"YB chill son, I got it," Murda said smoothly. YB was sweating with a crazy look in his face. "Trap you killed my mom and injured my little brother for life. Now it's your time."

"Fuck…you," Trap said spitting out blood in between deep breaths.

"I know," Murda said before he shot him thirteen times in the skull. As soon as he turned to leave, YB pulled out a knife and cut his eyes out and tongue.

"I'ma start a collection," YB said putting the items in his back pocket.

"Whatever makes you happy, son," Murda said as they both walked out.

***

Jamika was in her apartment doing her work on this Murda kid. She had his mugshot and to her, he was a little handsome.

Erica gave her so many unsolved murder cases but when she opened up the cases and obtained the DNA, the blood pattern analysis never added up because whoever committed these murders didn't leave no type of DNA. Not a fiber, semen, forensic nothing she could use to build a case on Murda.

She stood up in her robe, bra and panties under walking to her kitchen to make herself a cup of coffee.

Jamika had a feeling Erica was telling the truth because she was too scared, and she really wanted her brother out. She saw women and males like this every day, willing to rat to get their loved ones free.

Personally, Jamika hated rats. Her thing was if you do the crime, man up and do the time.

She planned to start tailing Murda tomorrow because she had a location on him. She needed something to nail him and if Erica was being 100% honest, then it would be easy to get something on him in no time.

Stacks sent her a goodnight text and she smiled. Her pussy got wet just thinking about him. She couldn't lie, she was in love with him. She was only scared to get hurt but she wanted to give him a try. She went to sleep thinking about her new mystery case criminal.

***

Queens, NY

Stacks was in his Queens auto body shop talking to VP. It was eleven at night. They just got done breaking the new shipment clean and placing it in different used cars they acted like they were selling but was using for stash spots.

"Take my Porsche tonight. I need you to fix the tire rods in the morning, so I'ma take your Benz truck," Stacks told

VP who was closing the trunk to the Acura RDX fill of bricks.

"Aight, son. Copy."

"Make sure everybody come pick up their shit. I'ma call Murda."

"Aight. That kid is making big moves. He's even known throughout my hood," VP stated putting on his backpack. He made it look as if he just came from work with his dirty machine uniform.

"Yeah he an official youngin' but I'ma head home," Stacks stated, walking out.

"Aight, boss. Right behind you."

Stacks hopped in VP's Benz and pulled off. Seconds after driving off, he heard a loud explosion causing him to look in his rearview mirror. He seen his Porsche in flames, with car parts being thrown everywhere.

Stacks couldn't believe what he just saw. Someone blew up his Porsche. He reversed down the block to see a white Lincoln truck speeding away.

"Fuck!" he screamed.

He rushed to VP, but he saw nothing except smoke and flames. He looked inside to see VP's body was burnt to a crisp. His arms and legs were under his driver's seat.

Stacks ran back into Benz, pulling off thinking how close that was to him losing his life. All he could think about was Freddy. He remembered the day he came to see him in the same GMC truck. There was no doubt in his mind. It was a war now.

Romell Tukes

Chapter Twenty
Manhattan, NY

Web couldn't believe today he was about to be a married man to the most beautiful woman he ever saw in his thirty-eight years on earth.

They were in a big catholic church full of guest, friends, and family members from both Web and Carmilla's sides of the family.

Web heard a knock at the door. He knew it wasn't Carmilla because she believed it was bad luck to see your soon to be groom before the wedding ceremony.

"Come in," he shouted as he saw Stacks walk inside in a fresh white custom tailor-made tuxedo. It was similar to the one Web wore but Web had real gold lines encrusted on his outfit with diamond cufflinks.

"Damn, B. Word is bond, you look Steve Harvey's stunt double, son," Stacks laughed, walking into a small dressing room.

"Thank you. Today marks a new phase in my life. I know I'm making the right choice," Web said.

"Follow your heart."

"I am. Thanks for being my best man. It says a lot," Web stated.

"Just make sure you do it for me when I marry Jamika's fine ass."

"Where is she? I saw y'all on social media. She is a beautiful woman," Web commented.

"She had to work but I told her about it. You know I told you the girl is a workaholic," Stacks said laughing as Web checked the time realizing it was time.

"Showtime. Come on, big homie," Web said leaving the room with Stacks on his heels.

***

Boyz II Men could be heard as Web stood next to the priest who was a Spanish man.

When everybody saw Carmilla come through the doors in tulle George chakra couture tiered gown, with Le Vian diamond and a laser-cut sequin. Rafael held her hand walking with her.

All of the five hundred people in the church upstairs and downstairs had made some type of sound when they saw how beautiful she looked even with a veil over her face.

Once she was face to face with Web, Rafael smiled and gave Web a nod of approval as he went to sit down surrounded by thirty goons.

"You look beautiful," he said uncovering her eyes.

"You do too," she said blushing as the priest began his service. After the priest made both of them say their vows and kissed, it was over the place went crazy.

There was a Royce Rolls limo waiting outside for them so they could take their private flight to Madrid, Spain for their honeymoon.

***

Madrid, Spain

Spain was beautiful. As soon as they got off the flight the temperate, clear, hot summer climate made them feels like they were in Miami.

The terrain and land were flat to dissected plateau surrounded by rugged hills and the Mediterranean Sea.

"This is beautiful, baby. Oh my," Carmilla said following him off the jet towards the Lincoln town car. The driver stood outside, waiting for them.

"Yeah I just hope no volcanoes erupt while we're down here," Web said looking into the mountains, while carrying their bags.

Carmilla was speaking Spanish to the personal driver.

"He said our resort awaits us," Carmilla said as Web placed two bags in the car.

"Aight lets go." He opened the door for her.

The driver drove through the inner city. It was beautiful seeing foreign women, cars, stores, tall glass skyscraper-buildings and businesses filled with beautiful Spanish women going in and out.

Once at their resort, they were escorted into the lobby filled with tourist from all over. Carmilla saw a large pod area and bar out back packed with people having fun.

"This is going to be free. I hear they have a nice restaurant on the other side and a club," Web stated as he gave Carmilla the room keys

"No clubbing for you, love. Especially tonight," she said sexually. She held the room keys in her hand as they made their way towards the elevator.

"I'm horny and as soon as we got upstairs, I want some dick. I haven't had sex in five years," she said being honest, causing his dick get hard.

"Perfect," he replied as they got off on the eighth floor to only see one room with double doors.

When they entered the suite, they attacked each other like two dogs that spent weeks away from each other.

Carmilla took off all his clothes and led him to the large bed in the middle of the room, filled with flowers, lights, mirrors, and candles.

Once he was naked, she slowly took off her dress, causing her nice perky breast popped out. She wanted to taste him first.

She slowly put the head of his twelve-inch dick in her warm mouth.

"You sure you can handle this?" Web said looking at her colorful eyes as she smiled and started to slowly suck his head.

Carmilla tightened her cheeks and started going faster and deeper as he moaned. Her mouth felt so good.

She caressed his balls with her hand as she was thrusting his dick down her throat. To Web, it was amazing how she was making his cock disappear in her mouth.

Web felt himself about to bust a nut, but he couldn't let her do him out this fast, so he pushed her lightly off.

He placed her on her back, kissing her soft lips then sliding down to her tan nipples, which were growing hard as he sucked them and traced his warm tongue around them.

Web swiftly and gracefully placed his tongue into her fat, wet pussy, which was shaved bald with a big size clit poking out of her thin smooth pussy lips. He could see she was dripping wet.

"Uhhhmmmmm shiiitttt," she moaned loudly as her hips moved with his tongue. He also slid his finger in her wetness.

Web made her climax twice before he knew it.

"Gimme me dick, papi," she demanded.

"Aight."

Web spread her legs apart like the letter V, as he entered her with no remorse. Once he was halfway in, it felt like her pussy had a stop sign. It was so tight.

"Oh," she gritted as he started to long stroke her wet pussy while sucking on her neck making her go crazy.

Web finally started to open her walls as she slowly pounded her wetness as his balls clapped on her ass cheeks.

"Ugghhh. Fuckkkk," she shouted taking that dick while gripping the white cotton sheet.

Web had her fired up now. She pumped her hips into him forcing his dick deeper into her little pussy.

"Take all of this dick. Say my name," Web shouted.

"Web. Papi. Web, I love youuu," she yelled as she moved her hips sideways in a circular motion as she continued to impale herself to his dick.

She wanted it doggy style after feeling him fill her up with his thick cum.

"Fuck me from behind," she said on all fours with her ass up and face down.

Her ass was wide, round, and soft as his hard dick was eager to be buried full-length into her tight pink pussy.

The head of his dick was pressing against her tight wet hole as she wiggled, her ass making it clap one cheek at a time for him.

Web entered her pussy until her tight pussy adjusted to the length and width of his dick. He grabbed her ass with two hands and started fucking her fast and hard as he drove his dick deeper with every thrust.

His dick was coming out coated with her cum.

"Ugghhh. Ohh yes. Give me more," she screamed as she came back-to-back.

He placed his thumb in her asshole, and she went crazy throwing her ass back loving the double penetration.

"I'm about to nut," Web said as his ass tightened, shooting another load in her.

Carmilla rode his dick for an hour and then sucked his dick for another hour. It was a long, hot, steamy night.

Romell Tukes

Chapter Twenty-One
White Plains, NY

Chris was parked behind White Plains projects in a Ford F-150 truck. He just got off of work with Jamika. They were working on so many new cases, they rarely had free time.

It was midnight and Chris was making his daily routine, picking up a couple of grams of coke to play with his nose. This coke habit was a recent one. With work, he had to get pissed test every month, but he been beating them with fake piss.

Him owing the Mafia $250,000 was so heavy on his mind, he couldn't even sleep or focus.

His coke dealer came to his window and tapped on the glass, Chris rolled down the window and handed the tall young black man in a hoodie two hundred dollars.

The dealer was so thirsty, he never asked if Chris was police or an informant. He just saw green.

"I'll see you tomorrow," the man said tossing three grams of coke in his lap before walking off.

Chris wasted no time as he pulled out a small mirror and put a line of cocaine on it then sniffed it, using a rolled-up dollar bill. Once he snorted, he leaned his head back on the headrest.

"Damn," he said putting everything in his armrest before heading home. The Mafia didn't care if Chris was a federal agent or judge. They were dangerous, and he knew this. He blamed his wife for introducing them to him.

Chris was thinking how he was going to come up with their money this time. He refused to go to Chelsea again. He had to come up with a new master plan to save his ass and career.

***

Bushwick Ave

Murda just arrived at Stacks auto body shop in a Ford Expedition and parked it in the car lot with all the other cars.

Since killing Trap, things had been a little quiet, which was how Murda liked it because the money was rolling in.

Murda walked towards the back to the office were Stacks told him to meet him

"Murda, what's good, playboy?" Stacks greeted.

"What's up? I see y'all got a busy day in this joint," Murda said looking outside the office to see his employees working hard on cars parked all over the garage.

"Yeah but you should invest your money, kid. Running around in a Bentley with no legit job or business is a red flag," Stacks said looking at him.

"I'm in the process of opening a sneaker store in the mall. I just gotta get my business license," said Murda.

"Good. Smart man. Your boys came to pick up your shipment this morning," Stack said.

"I know. I was just dropping off the money. There's $850,000 in the trunk of the Expedition parked outside," he replied.

"Ok. Take the Infiniti parked next to it. I'ma have someone pick it up tonight," Stacks stated.

"Cool I'ma get out of here. Once again, thanks for everything."

"Sure, no problem," Stacks said about to make some business calls.

***

Jamika was watching Murda's every move as he went into Stacks auto shop and came out.

"What the fuck is going on?" she said to herself sitting behind the tints of a gray Toyota Camry.

She had been tailing him for days, thanks to Erica giving her his location where they rested their heads.

Since tailing him, she hadn't saw anything out of the ordinary, except him riding around in a Bentley and going to almost every hood in BK.

He was well liked, she could tell by the way people acted around him. He was someone well respected.

Jamika couldn't figure out why would he choose to come to this auto shop instead of all the other ones around Brooklyn.

Now she saw him pulling out in a new nice Infiniti, leaving the car he arrived in, which confused her.

She started to tail him again making his way downtown. All she could think about was Stacks and if Murda knew the man she was truly falling in love with.

Jamika knew people's cars needed fixing, so she didn't want to over think it, even though she felt something was wrong.

***

Freddy's daughter Kate was in town visiting from Kentucky, with her daughter, who just turned five.

Kate was cute, tall, dark hair, no ass and flat chested but her porn star face made up for all of her flaws.

She was in the supermarket doing some food shopping with her daughter so they could cook a big Italian meal tonight at her father mansion.

Kate grew up around the mafia her whole life. At twenty-six-years-old, she had her life in order. She was married to a lawyer, she was a bail bondsman assistant, and she was a good mother.

"Mommy, mommy, mommy. Can I have this?" her daughter asked grabbing a pack of gum off the register shelf.

"Sure."

After paying for everything, she pushed the cart to her father's Buick Regal. She loaded the bags into the back and placed her daughter in her car seat.

"Can we go to the park?" her cute daughter asked with her two front teeth missing.

"Maybe," Kate said looking in the sky to see the sun was shining bright outside today.

Pulling out of the shopping center lot, she called her father on speaker as she drove through the streets of Brooklyn, a place she grew up and love and hated.

Kate stopped at a red light as her daughter sang the Taylor Swift's song that played on her personal MP3 player.

Before the light hit green, gunfire started to ring out as the Buick's windows shattered everywhere.

Kate was shot twice in the head and six times in her lower torso. Her daughter screamed and tried to cower down, but a spray of bullets hit the little girl four times in piercing her lungs and liver, eventually killing her before help could arrive.

Stacks raced off in a Hyundai sedan doing ninety down a Main Street. He had been watching Kate for hours since he saw Freddy pick her up from JFK airport.

Months ago, before VP died, he placed a GPS tracker under Freddy's car and Stacks always kept track of him, just in case he would try anything dumb.

Chapter Twenty-Two
King County Hospital

Erica was working a double shift today, just to get some overtime and get away from Murda. Since she had been working for Jamika as a rat, she been uncomfortable around him.

"Yo, Erica. What's up, girl?" her friend and co-worker Star greeted, approaching her desk in the workstation in the middle of the second floor.

"Star what's going on? I like your hair. The blue thing really brings out your dark, smooth skin," Erica said as Star pulled up a rolling chair next to her.

"Thanks. I love it also," she replied sounding cocky.

Star was a Jamaican chick from Flatbush. She was twenty-seven and beautiful. At five foot four, she was super thick with big titties and big legs to match her fat ass. She was dark skin with good hair she always dyed and was always rocking the latest fashions.

"There is so much going on in my hood, Erica. It's crazy," Starr stated taking a deep breath.

"Like what?" Erica asked scrolling through her Facebook page with her long, manicured nails.

"My cousin's baby daddy, Trap was murdered a couple of weeks ago girl, and they found this niggas body in Mount Vernon projects with his eyes and tongue cut out," Star revealed, shaking her head.

Star brought Erica all the juicy gossip in Brooklyn. She kept her in tune with the streets. She was worse than the Wendy Williams show. Star was a real nosey hood rat that talked about anything anybody.

This was the reason why Erica kept her private life away from work because she knew Star would have all her business in the hospital.

When Erica heard the name Trap, it rang a bell in her head, but it wasn't clicking.

"Damn Star mama. I'm sorry to hear that", Erica said it with her Spanish Brooklyn accent.

"Yeah word is some big shot nigga from East New York, named Murda did it. They say he ain't nothing to fuck with," Star said in a low pitch as Erica zoned out just hearing her boyfriend's name. "Erica! Erica! You ok?" Star asked.

"Oh yeah."

"Damn, you just zoned the fuck out on me, girl," Star said waving at some of their co-workers coming into work.

"I gotta go use the bathroom. I'ma be right back, ma," Erica said taking her purse with her, not trusting Star's grimy ass. Star told her how she used to get down.

Erica rushed in the bathroom and called Jamika, informing her she has something to tell her ASAP. She agreed to me Erica Sunday morning.

Erica remembered where she heard the name Trap from now. Weeks ago, she overheard Murda on the phone with YB telling him to find a nigga name Trap and he was a dead man.

She sat on the toilet and took three deep breaths. She couldn't believe she was doing this, but she had to do what she had to do for Troy.

***

Later that Night

Stacks had just got done fucking the shit out of Jamika and she was out cold. Lately, they've been spending a lot of time at each other's places. He was ready to ask her to move in with him.

He looked over at her to see how sexy she was asleep. He had to admit she was everything he wanted in a woman.

Stacks got up and climbed out the bed to take a piss, but as he walked down her dark hall in his boxers, he saw Jamika's room she used for work, which she always locked when he came over.

Seeing this room unlocked for the first time, made him want to be nosey. Looking back to make sure he could still hear Jamika's snores. He made his way in her private room.

The small size room looked like an office with file cabinets, a big desk, two laptop computers, a lamp, papers all over the place, and a fax machine.

Stacks saw a small tape recorder on the top of the documents, without hesitation he pressed the play button. He listened to it and it was a female telling her about murders that happened in East New York as Jamika questioned her. Stacks was confused when he heard Jamika asking the Spanish women questions about some murders.

He opened her draw to see a Glock 17 handgun that only police had, but what he saw behind it gave him chills. He saw an FBI badge with Jamika's name on it and he saw her work ID at the White Plains federal build.

"FUCK," Stacks said scared, as he continued to listen to the tape recorder and looking through some of the documents to see photos under the stacks of paper.

When he saw the niggas face on the first four photos, his heart started to race as he saw pictures of Murda hopping out his Bentley.

Still listening to the tape recorder, he heard Jamika call the Spanish woman, Erica as she kept mentioning Murda's name.

Stacks continued to look through the papers and file cabinets to see if she had anything on him and Web, but she didn't.

Twenty minutes later, he went back to bed thinking about Jamika and her status. He could never put her as an agent, but he didn't understand why she would tell him she worked for the state if she was a federal agent.

All he could think about was if he was on her hitlist and if this was a set up. He went to sleep that with one eye open.

Chapter Twenty-Three
Rikers Island Jail

YB was in the three building on the dayroom phone, speaking to Murda telling him his bail the judge gave him for a gun charge he caught two weeks ago coming from club Nova.

Murda told him he was going to send Rihanna to post his bail in two days. When YB got off the phone with Murda, he felt better knowing he would be getting out because Rikers Island was no joke. Niggas was getting their face ripped left and right.

Two weeks ago, when he came to five main in the three building, he snatched a cell from a Bronx nigga and beat him into a coma, stomping his face into the bars with his Timbs.

Inmates wore regular cloths in the famous Rikers Island jail and some wore jewelry as long as they were ready to go to war for it.

YB went and sat down in front of his TV as seventeen inmates all sat behind him quietly. They all tuned into Love & Hip Hop.

"Let me holler at you, young blood," an older cat named Black from Cypress projects stated. He used to run with the A-team back in the day until it caught him two life sentences in the state.

"What's popping, OG?" YB said walking to the back where Black was sitting reading his Quran.

"Sit down, real quick. Let me school you to something, young wolf. You have to be humble. Anybody can be a gangsta or a bully but a real gangsta is a thinker and one who is humble. Just because we from Brooklyn, don't make us more of a man," Black said as YB looked in his dark cold eyes, not knowing the old head had over forty bodies.

"That's a fact," YB stated, looking out the day room window to see a cute redbone CO chick blow him a kiss. She was on his line. She was from Brooklyn and feeling his swag.

"You remember an older dude from your hood named Stacks?" Black asked.

"I believe so," YB stated remembering Murda speaking his name a couple of times.

"Before he become the main nigga, I schooled him. I raised him and every month, he made sure my account stays fat and my family was good, but I see a lot of him in you, son, but you just gotta slow down," Black said firmly.

"Stacks hood rich or something?"

"Hood rich? Kid this nigga got more money than Oprah and Magic Johnson," Black laughed, standing up.

"Damn, son. Word to mother, that's crazy," YB said thinking about Stacks as they called a rec move so inmates could go outside.

***

Madrid, Spain

Web was on his way downstairs to check out after spending two and a half weeks in Spain, which was amazing.

Him and Carmilla went on jet skis, boat cruises, skydiving, swimming with sharks, fancy dinners, shopping, clubbing in the inner city and of course rough hot sex on new beaches.

Web forgot his I.D. so he took the elevator back upstairs in a rush hoping they don't miss their private flight back home. He brought her a nice mini mansion in Long Island. He was sure she would like it.

As soon as he stepped foot in the room, he heard Camila yelling in Spanish to someone on the phone in the bathroom

Being nosey, Web pulled out his phone and moved closer to the door recording her. Web never heard Carmilla yell and she was going in on whoever she was speaking to on the other line.

After a full minute of yelling, Carmilla told the caller she would explain everything when she got back. She hung up and flushed the toilet as if she was using the bathroom

Web ran off and acted as if he was packing up.

"Oh, baby. Hey, I thought you went downstairs. How long was you standing there?" Carmilla said with a fake smile as her silk robe was opening showing her flat stomach and sexy body.

"Yeah I just now came in. I was looking for this," Web pulled out his ID from his slacks he wore last night.

"I am finished packing up, baby. I love you, papi," she stated as he rushed back out thinking if she was on the phone with another nigga or ex.

"Love you too," he said closing the door behind him as his mind was racing.

***

Lil Italy, NY

Stacks pulled up to Web's new club, impressed. It was big, classy, and right in the middle of the Mafia headquarters.

Stacks had to admit, Web had some big balls moving a club in Joe's area. He could only imagine how sick the mob was that Web violated to this level.

Since the beef was on, Stacks traveled with a crew of shooters in an SUV. They parked down the block watching Stacks every move as he climbed out the pearl white CLS 600 Benz that had the body kit and 362 horsepower.

Stacks killing Freddy's daughter was a big plus on his scoreboard. He saw the killing on the news, but he had no remorse for killing the baby. It was war time and in war, anything goes.

He walked in the lounge giving his crew a nod, letting them know he was ok.

Stacks made his way to the back where Web was awaiting him. The now empty lounge would be in full effect in four hours for happy hour at five o'clock.

"Yoo what's good, big homie?" Web greeted Stacks as he walked in his office in a pair of Gucci shorts and a Gucci t-shirt.

"We got a problem," Stack said as Web smile turned into a frown.

"What now?"

"This chick Jamika is a fucking FBI agent," Stacks said pacing back and forth.

"You're fucking kidding, man! Hold on, is she an informant? C.I? Rat? Mole?" Web asked.

"No, she is an agent. I saw her badge and everything. She's trying to build a case on the kid Murda I was telling you about. The one who is moving all of our shit," Stacks informed him.

"How the fuck did she so close to home? What did she have on us?" Web asked with a concerned look.

"That's the odd part, my nigga. She had nothing on us and the only thing she had on him was photos and a chick name Erica telling on him about some murders. She seemed like she knew a lot about our guy," Stacks said

"If Jamika looks deep enough, she's going put two and two together then what?"

"That's a fact. I'm on it."

"Stacks, I got a real honest question for you and I need you to keep it real," Web asked seriously.

"Yeah, anything."

"How do you really feel about this girl Jamika?" Web asked leaning back in his chair.

"I love her, but I'm married to the streets," he replied sharply.

"Aight so I am let you handle it how you handle it, because I feel Carmilla isn't being honest with something. Now I gotta do some serious research on her so I'ma be a little busy these next couple of days," Web stated as if he was in deep thought.

"Damn so the honeymoon was bad?"

"Nah. It was amazing, but I think she got secrets or I'm just overreacting."

"You think she's cheating already or got another man?"

"To be honest, I don't know yet, but I am finding out. *Trust No Bitch* by Cash put a nigga on game for real," Web laughed.

"Where she at now?"

"D.C."

"Give it some time, bro. Y'all just got married. Give her the benefit of the doubt but I gotta go. Before I forget, I killed Freddy's daughter and granddaughter so it's lit," Stack stated.

"Good," Web smiled.

Romell Tukes

Chapter Twenty-Four
White Plains, NY

Chris was driving home from working with many thoughts running through his mind, as he was high off coke.

The past couple of months have been hell for Chris. Work was taking a toll on him because he hadn't been able to steal money or drugs from criminals or the basement storage area because he was being watched by the higher ups.

To make matters worse, him and his wife were on the line of a divorce because Chris' vicious habits. It was to the point where they slept in different rooms just so they don't have to see each other.

Chris went as far as pawning his ring two days ago for $20,000 hoping to triple his money in Atlantic City so he could pay Freddy something, but he lost it all in less than five minutes.

He even went as low as asking his co-worker Jamika for money. When she asked him what he needed it for, he told her college loans and bills.

She agreed to give him $10,000 tomorrow to help him, unaware of any of his bad habits.

Chris pulled down his quiet, dark block and parked his truck in the driveway next to Chelsea's BMW X5. Chris was thinking how much he could get if he was to steal his wife's car and take it to a chop shop to sell.

As he climbed out of the truck with his workbag in his hand, a large piece of metal pipe, slammed into Chris' temple, knocking him clean out on his lawn. Freddy's goons dragged his body into a big blue van parked in the middle of the street.

***

Chris woke up several minutes later with half of his head and face in serious pain. Once he clearly got his vision, he realized he was cuffed up hands and ankles in the back of an empty van with no seats, just full of big white boys with mean faces and guns drawn.

"You've been ducking my calls, Chris. I don't like when people dodge me," a voice said from the passenger seat as he turned around to lock Chris in his eyes.

"Freddy, man, I've been busy at work, but all of this is uncalled for," Chris said as he looked at the six big wrestlers waiting for him to make any move.

"Pull over, right there," Freddy told the driver.

"Where are we? What's going on?" Chris asked seeing out the window that they were somewhere on a bridge.

"Bring him out," Freddy stated climbing out. His goon snatched Chris out like a rag doll by his ankles and arms as he yelled for them to stop. "Hang him."

Freddy watched four of his goons toss Chris' body over the Brooklyn Bridge, holding him by his ankles

"Fred. Please, no!" Chris cried, dangling off the side of the Brooklyn Bridge.

"Chris, when will I have my $250,000? I've been patient my friend."

"I'ma have it for you in two weeks or less. Please, Freddy. I'm just waiting on my wife's loan check to arrive."

"Ok Chris, but next time I won't be so nice. I'll be back in two weeks. Pull him up and leave him here," Freddy said climbing back in the van with his soldiers pulling off.

Chris laid on the floor, still cuffed up and scared to death, especially now that cars started to ride by.

Ten minutes later, as it started to rain, an old man saw him on the floor and helped him wondering how he got there like that.

***

Downtown, BK

Web was in his restaurant he had open two years ago and was doing very well. It was a Latina & Soul food spot that serviced every type of food you could think of.

"Kimmy, can I speak to you for a minute?" Web stated as he saw her take a customer's order.

"Yes, boss," she said, nervously thinking he was about to fire her because he never said a word to her the whole year of working here

She was a cute Dominican chick from Harlem with a two-year-old son to raise as a single mother.

"Close the door behind you and have a seat," Web instructed, sitting down.

"Ok," She said in her strong Spanish accent. She only been in a states five years.

"Whatever we discuss in here, is between me and you," Web stated as she nodded her head yes, thinking he was going to try to have sex with her. She hoped so because she was really feeling him

"Our little secret will always be mine," she said as she started to unbutton her blouse shirt.

"What are you doing?" he asked as he pulled out his iPhone.

"I thought you wanted to…" she paused when she looked at the awkward look on his face, feeling stupid. "Oh, I'm sorry," she stated.

"It's ok, but I need you to listen to this conversation. It's in Spanish," he said handing her his phone as he put it on speaker.

Kimmy was listening and making weird facial expressions.

"Whoever the woman was speaking to, she was telling him she needs more time and she didn't have much to go off of yet. She also told him she is the FBI agent who does her job and when she goes back to DC, she will speak to the boss."

Web looked at her as if she was a disease.

"Are you sure that's what you heard?" he asked.

"I promise you, papi. Word for word, the woman is an FBI agent, sounding as if she is working on a case of someone important," she said.

"Thank you I am going to make sure you get a two thousand dollar bonus this paycheck."

"Wow, thank you, Mr. Web," Kimmy said standing to leave.

Web was sick hearing Carmilla was an agent. How could he be so blind by beauty? He wondered if Stacks and his situation was somehow connected but then he thought about Rafael. Does he know his daughter is a federal agent? Nothing was making sense to Web.

He left the restaurant going to his Long Island home to clear his head and check on Carmilla, trying to see if she would give him any signs.

Chapter Twenty-Five
Wingate Park

Murda was sitting in the park under the gazebo waiting on Stacks to arrive because he said he needed to speak to him.

It was nine at night and Murda had to go pick up some money from Gates Ave and go holler at Tookie.

Things were going great. Gunna was back to walking and driving again, but lately he's been hanging around the projects to much and Murda been trying to warn him, but he wouldn't listen.

Erica was acting funny. The two hadn't had sex in weeks. She had been really distant lately and he had no clue why.

He saw a Benz pull up behind his Bentley with HD lights. Stacks hopped out in some gym gear showing his define chest and big arms. Murda was impressed. For an old nigga, he kept in shape.

"Murda, what's good? Peep game, let me get your phone for a second."

"Huh?"

"I'ma give it right back," Stacks said as he took Murda's phone and put it inside his car.

Murda watched him with a confused look, not sure as to why he just did that. It was almost as if he thought Murda was wired or something.

"What's that about?" Murda asked when Stacks walked back over to him.

"We have a big problem. Do you know a chick by the name of Erica?" Stacks asked looking him right in his eyes

"Yeah, that's my wifey. What's going on? Is she ok? Murda asked sounding worried.

147

"Damn it," Stacks shouted, pissed off.

"What's wrong?"

"She's telling an FBI agent everything about some murders and your dealings. She's working for her," Stacks said as Murda's face went sour. He couldn't believe what he was hearing.

"This shit is crazy. How did you hear all of this? Are you positive it was Erica?" he said not wanting to believe his lover was working for them people.

"The FBI agent is a chick I'm dealing with. I had no clue she was an agent until I saw your photos and heard a recorded conversation of Erica telling her everything. I'm talking shit that could land you and me in prison."

"She knows about you too?" Murda asked, sick. His girl was now a rat.

"No not yet and we need to change up some shit. First get rid of that Bentley. Get rid of that phone, and get rid of Erica," Stacks stated as he froze.

"Just give me some time. I'ma handle it, bro," Murda stated.

"You handle it, or I will," Stacks warned, walking off leaving him standing there looking dumbfounded.

Murda couldn't believe Erica was trying to bring him down but for what?

Then it hit him. Her brother Troy.

He really loved Erika but now she crossed a line and there was no coming back. Murda couldn't let her bring and his people down. He refused to.

This was the part of the game he hated of course, but he knew it was a cold game. Murda's first stop was getting rid of his phone and Bentley.

***

Court St, BK

Joe was looking at pictures and documents of Web and Chris while a private investigator sat across from him. "Ain't this some fucking shit. Mr. Web's brother is a fucking dirty pig who owes Freddy his life," Joe smiled, seeing documents stating the two were blood brothers.

"Yeah this is a blessing and a curse, I guess," the P.I stated.

"I didn't ask you that. You can leave. I'll have my assistant out front write your check," Joe said looking at all the info he had on Web now.

"Thank you," the P.I. said, leaving. Now was Joe's time to come up with a vicious get back. It was about time he showed him who really ran New York.

***

Bushwick Ave

YB was sitting on the dark block across the street from Stacks auto shop in a blue Honda. He was watching Stacks lock up his shop before he climbed in a Benz.

Since YB been out on bail from the Island, he been watching Stacks very closely. Ever since the old head Black informed him of Stacks being a millionaire, YB couldn't kick it out his head.

Last week, Murda told him he had to meet Stacks at Wingate Park and YB followed him. That same night, he began trailing Stacks, never losing sight of him and tonight wouldn't be any different. Later, he patiently watched Stacks load drugs into the car.

YB was a jack boy. He couldn't help it. Even if he was up, if someone had something he wanted, he was going to take it.

He couldn't tell Murda about this or let him find out he was doing this because Murda and Stacks had a good relationship, but he could care less about the nigga.

Once the taillights of the Benz was all the way down the block, YB hopped out the stolen Honda and made his way to the Nissan truck.

YB was a professional car thief, so it took him two seconds to get inside and disarm the car.

Inside the car, he looked in the back to see nothing but when he lifted the floor panel, he saw bricks on top of bricks.

YB knew he just hit the big score. Without hesitation, he hopped in the car and pulled off knowing he was about to be a rich man.

There was no way he was going to sell bricks in Brooklyn. He knew Stacks was connected and he didn't want Murda to get wind of what he just did.

Murda was his best friend but he knew Murda would've felt some type of way. He just robbed a nigga he fucked with but YB was a true Brooklyn nigga. There was no such thing as loyalty to him.

Chapter Twenty-Six
Long Island, NY

"Hey baby. Good morning." Carmilla walked into their beautiful marble floor stainless steel kitchen in a Miu Miu business suit with her long hair in a bun looking beautiful.

"What's up ma?" Web said drinking a cup of dark coffee with no sugar, reading a newspaper waiting on the maid to arrive.

"Why you sound so flat, papi?" she asked, rubbing his shoulders trying to lighten him up

"Sometimes things don't always be as they seem, but how do you like your new job?" he asked.

"It's ok, I guess. The City Hall is ok until I found something good," she said not feeling his vibe, so she walked off into the living room.

The mansion was 6,178 square feet with pullout doors, a basement gym, four car garage, six bedrooms, four bathrooms, living room area with all white thick carpet and white leather chairs.

Carmilla found a new job in New York just so she could stay in there instead of working in D.C.

"I don't really understand your hours yet, but I want to do something special for you tonight," he said.

"Oh, wow. I'll make sure I'm home early, daddy," she happily stated, ready to head to work.

As soon as she left, Web rushed out behind her when he heard her car speed down the driveway.

Web hopped inside of his BMW M2. He couldn't use his Wraith or Maybach because it would stick out like a sore thumb for his mission.

After his employee told him Carmilla was an FBI agent, he been very wary of her.

Web tried to reason with himself that Carmilla wasn't an agent or this person who is trying to bring his life and empire down.

Then it was the marriage, the love at first sight and their connection. He wondered if it was real or was it a lie.

When he saw her Land Rover Range SV coupe taillights, he kept a good distance on her as she rode through East Hampton.

It was nice, hot and sunny today, but Web was still confused as he saw Carmilla riding into Jones Beach parking lot.

The beach was packed this morning but Carmilla was the only one there dressed in a suit until he saw a tall white woman in a suit and a short stocky dude, wearing a suit also looking out of place standing next to their Genesis G70.

Carmilla handed the man a brown envelope with papers in it as they started talking as if they weren't agreeing. The white woman tried to claim both of them down.

Web saw gun holsters poking out of their shirts, so it wasn't hard to put two and two together. They wear cops. He saw the cop hand her back the envelope and Carmilla threw it at his chest and walked off.

When Camila pulled off, he saw the other two cops yelling at each other. Web used his goggles to look closer at the two cops to see a FBI license plate on their car and FBI badges on their necks.

"God damn," Web said as Carmilla was speeding his way. He tried to lean back in his seats. Luckily his car had a van in front of him as he rode past and the Genesis wasn't too far behind her.

Web knew for a fact new Carmilla was the Feds, but now he needed to know what her agenda was. He pulled out of his parking spot and followed Carmilla as she made her way to City Hall to go to work.

***

Hours Later

With the house lights dim, little rose petals everywhere and lit cherry and peach Yankee Candles, the house had a strong sweet scent.

He wore a red Balenciaga suit with a tie. He had been cooking for hours. Tonight, he wanted to cater to his wife so she could know what type of man he was.

Checking his watch, he knew she should be in any minute, so he waited in the dining room for her to come in.

"Babe, where you at? Why does it smell so good in here?" Carmilla stated walking into the house sniffing, the roses and candles.

"Surprise," he smiled.

"Oh, nice. This is a nice setup," she said looking at all of the food on the table and trays with lids on them.

"Have a seat, my Queen." Web pulled out a second chair for her, taking her blazer and purse off her and tossing it on the coat rack.

"You make me feel so good, papi," she said in her Spanish accent.

"I got a surprise for you, boo. Close your eyes. I am tie you up and blindfold you," he said as she closed her eyes with her pussy drenched

"Mmmmm naughty," she stated as he placed a blindfold over her. He then put her hands behind her back, putting cuffs on them. He did the same thing to her ankles. "Where you get cuffs from baby? They feel real and tight," she asked unable to see what was going on.

"Carmilla, who the fuck are you?" he questioned, now pulling off her blindfold.

"What are you talking about? I'm your wife," she said dumbfounded as she saw him lift a tray top.

"Bitch, who are you?" Web asked again, picking up glock 45 fully loaded and pointed it at her as she showed no fear and took a deep breath.

"How did you find out so fast?"

"Carmilla I'm not dumb but why me? Why go this far to set me up?" he asked.

"Web, I'm a federal agent. I work for the headquarters in D.C.," she responded.

"How and your father is Rafael? Is he even your real father?"

"Yes, but Web, I have something to tell you that's very important. Please listen, my father is the one who made me build a case on you. My father is a snake and a rat. I never was supposed to fall in love with you or marry you. I was supposed to get close enough to you to have enough information to put under the jail, then my pops was next. You have to believe me," she cried.

"Your father is doing this for what? I don't understand and you played me. You had me fall in love with you to only be setting me up the whole time?" Web said now getting pissed off thinking about it.

"I don't know what my father is up to but after he gave us you, he was next. I'm sorry, Web. I was doing my job. I didn't mean to fall in love with you. It wasn't a part of the plan."

"Shut the fuck up," he said, slapping her hard with an open hand.

"Please, Web listen they have nothing on you. They only what my father gave me. You're very smart but my father has it out for you and the Feds do too now," she said. "Since I came to New York, my headquarters thought it would be good to work with the FBI up here, but they never even heard of you. They are thirsty to build whatever I can give them. I told them I don't have nothing on you yet except your record, which is clean. You have a couple of tickets and business records." she said, and he believed her.

"I should kill you right now but I'm not. I don't know why because mark my words if I find out you're lying bitch, I'ma chop your little sexy body in pieces," Web stated pulling out a long needle as if she was about to get a flu shot.

"What's that?" she asked as her eyes widened. "Web I'm in love with you still," she said before he stuck the needle in her arm, and she blacked out.

Chapter Twenty-Seven
New Rock, NY

Murda was on the highway in his new Ford Mustang Shelby GT350 all black with tints. Since he sold his Bentley, he been low key in his Shelby.

He was coming from New Rock Movie Theater with Erica who was in his passenger seat, sleeping.

When Stacks told him weeks ago about Erica snitching on him, he been playing her very close. He paused everything on all of his drug operations until he was able to figure this shit out, but he knew Erica was moving very funny and nervous.

Tonight, was the night he been plotting for a while. He planned to find out everything from Erica one-way or another.

***

Twenty Minutes Later

Murda just pulled into the City of Peekskill train station lot. It was eleven at night, so the area was dark and empty.

The Hudson River was directly behind them. He looked over to his right and woke Erica up at her sleep

"What? We home?" she said grumpy.

"Get the fuck out," he said in a serious tone. She looked at him, trying to figure out why he was so rude.

"Where are we and what's wrong with you?" she said as she saw him pull a gun out from under his seat

"Get out," Murda repeated, putting the gun to her head as she quickly opened the door and stepped out.

Murda hopped out and rushed towards her around the car and started to pat her down for wires.

"What are you doing?" she asked as if he just went crazy for no reason.

"Who are you working for? What do they know?" He asked her sternly staring at her puppy dog eyes.

"I d-don't know what you're talking about, babe. Please, you're scaring me," she stuttered.

Murda placed the tip of the barrel to her forehead and applied pressure.

"Don't make me ask your snake ass again, bitch."

"Her name is Jamika, but I only did it to get Troy out. Murda, I'm sorry. I love you. I wasn't thinking straight," she cried.

"What did you tell her?" he asked.

"I had to tell her everything about the murders I knew about and money I had. I'm sorry. She knows everything. What was I supposed to do?"

"Fuck you, you stupid muthafucker," he shouted. He was madder at himself for even letting Erica know his personal lifestyle affairs. He was sloppy at times. He openly spoke in front of her and allowed her to see a lot of money and drugs.

"I can take back what I told her," she lied. She spotted the train coming from the other side of the River.

"It's too late, Erica. You crossed me."

"It was a mistake. Please, let me make it right," she said.

"Sorry," Murda said sadly before he shot her three times in the head then watched her body slump on his car door.

Murda dragged her body thirty feet to the train tracks and left her there, as the emergency blockers came down with flashing red lights letting people know a train was near.

Murda climbed in his car and watched the train approach, blowing its loud horn thinking someone was playing on the tracks because the train was too close to stop.

When the train drove over her body, Murda saw her legs fly four feet in the air towards the grass before he pulled up and left.

***

FBI

Jamika was sitting at her office desk reading over Erica's police report on how they found her with three shots to the skull and her lower body detached from her upper torso, which was crushed by a train.

The photos were too gruesome to look at but she felt as if it was her fault. She made her dig more and more into Mafia affairs so she would have a solid case.

There was no doubt in her mind that Murda killed her or had her killed.

Jamika twirled the ink pen in her mouth wondering if he found out she was bringing her information or found something out and had to cover his ass, so he killed the love of his life.

Erica told her how dangerous he was, and she was down-playing the situation. Now she knew firsthand she was dealing with a monster.

She called her partner Chris' phone, only to get his voicemail. She wanted to see if he wanted to go to MDC Brooklyn to speak with Troy, but she couldn't get a hold of him for the sixth day.

Lately, she been seeing Chris act totally different and looking spooked as if he was on drugs.

Jamika grabbed her badge, gun, and purse and left to see her male coworker staring at her ass as always. She was the only black woman in the building, so they treated her as if she was a piece of meat and she hated that.

"Hey, Jamika. Where are you going? Let's go have a drink tonight. I bet you like Henny," a fat agent said.

"I'm sure your wife won't like that, Peter Griffin. You should find your dick before you try to set up dates," Jamika said as a gang of agents started laughing.

***

MDC, Brooklyn

Jamika flashed her badge when she walked in the over-crowded lobby at Brooklyn federal hold over.

Jamika thought all the good men were either dead or in jail, but Stacks proved that myth wrong. He was so perfect, she was scared.

Troy knocked on the door and walked in with a sad, crazy look on his face as if he was on the edge of hanging up.

"Troy how are you doing?" she asked as he pulled out a chair and sat down ice grilling her.

"My sister was just found murdered. How would you feel if you were in my shoes?" he asked smartly.

Jamika wanted to tell him she could never be in his shoes because she would never to come jail and rat or have someone rat for her.

"I'm sorry to hear that, but I'm still here to help. Before your sister was murdered, she gave me enough information to build a strong case on Murda, so I am still trying to get you out on an early release. If you can help me with some more info on him or his crew, it could help on your behalf," she said looking at his smirk.

"I told you when you first booked me, I wasn't a rat and I am standing on that. I'm on Blood time. They see some fishy shit in my PSI, docket sheet, or sentencing transcript, are you going to save me from being stabbed to death?"

"You make deals at your own risk. Your sister is dead trying to help get you out and you're not a snitch now?"

"I'm out, if I hear something, I'll call or email you," Troy said storming out the room pissed off. Jamika sat there wondering if he was high off K-2 or something that inmates tripped out off of.

Romell Tukes

Chapter Twenty-Eight
Bushwick Ave

Stacks sat in his auto shop office reviewing the camera from weeks ago, when his car filled with bricks was stolen.

The next day after the car was stolen, he arrived at work and pistol whipped two of his employees who were now filing a lawsuit against him, because he thought they had parts in the robbery.

The beef with the Mafia was getting crazy around the city. His main clients were coming up missing, found dead, or seriously injured by Freddy and his goons. The war was on.

Stacks been so busy, he didn't have time to find out who responsible for robbing his shit. The more he looked at the video, the more he thought his mind was playing tricks on him.

He played the footage again in slow motion trying to get a good look at the robber who wore no mask, with a death wish.

"Get the fuck outta here. It can't be this little nigga," Stacks shouted to himself as he zoomed in on none other than YB, creeping into his car lot.

Stacks knew he must've been watching him because for him to get that lucky and hit the first try, was rare.

He paused on YB's face and wondered if Murda had anything to do with this. He quickly erased the thought from his mind just as fast as it entered.

He knew Murda was a stand-up kid, but YB was a different type of breed. He never liked the kid from the jump because he knew he was sneaky.

A sneak thief was like a rapist to him because he was from Brooklyn where a nigga would rob you in your face and walk past you the next day wearing your shit.

Stacks couldn't let this slide. He was never a sucker nigga and he knew he had to show YB firsthand. He only hoped his relationship with Murda would remain the same with whatever the outcome turned out to be.

***

White Plains, NY

Freddy sat in the back of the Rolls Royce Phantom smoking a cigar as two of his guards watch Chris and Chelsea's home.

Freddy was waiting for Chris to come back because Joe wanted him dead since he found out Web was his brother.

He went for the next best thing, which was his brother, who was in debt already, so he was now a walking dead man.

With so much going on with the war with Stacks and the Blacks, Freddy forgot about Joe's situation with Web.

Freddy saw Chelsea go out with her coworkers to have drinks and she left her two beautiful daughters at home with a babysitter who lived on the same block.

"I'm getting bored. Come on, I'm no babysitter. I am sending this nigga a message and this nigga lover," Freddy snapped. He was mad because Chelsea never gave him the time of day.

Freddy and his two goons walked up to Chris' and rang his doorbell twice. When he heard a young girls voice, he pulled out his pistol with a silencer.

The cute teenage white girl with braces on her teeth, opened a door wearing tight jeans that were unbuckled and a blouse with her long pink nipples hard as if she was about to fuck. A young teenage black boy came up behind her with no shirt on and shorts with a hard on as if he was just getting some head.

"You looking for someone? If not, please, we're busy," she said with a small cum drip on the side of mouth.

"Little rude bitch," Freddy said with his hands and gun behind his back.

"Don't speak to my girl like that," the tall skinny black kid said as Freddy and his goons laughed.

"It must be a lot of jungle fever around here, but I'ma do the both of you a favor, just so you won't destroy the white race."

PSST.

PSST.

PSST.

PSST.

PSST.

PSST.

Freddy shot both of them as he walked in the house while his guards pumped more shells into the horny teenagers.

The first room upstairs was a double bunk with two little girls.

"Mommy," one of the little girls said waking up out her sleep.

"Daddy," the other little girl said.

"Shhh. They'll be with you soon." Freddy started shooting both of the little girls.

Freddie walked out the house smiling, feeling like going to a classy gentlemen's club in Nyack, where he brought pussy at daily.

***

Five Minutes Later

Jamika pulled up to Chris' driveway to check on him and to see what was going on because he had been M.I.A for too long.

She found it odd that his car nor his wife's car wasn't there, but their home door was open.

Jamika had a funny feeling about this as she walked towards the front door that was open. She saw a leg sticking out from behind it halfway.

"Chris. Chelsea," Jamika called, opening the door to feel something behind it.

Once she walked near, she saw a teenage girl and boy, lying in puddles of blood.

Jamika called it in on her walkie talkie and pulled out her work gun, just in case the killer was still in the house, unaware she rode past him minutes ago.

After calling in, she ran upstairs remembering Chris' cute daughters, hoping they were sleep. When she opened the door, she almost lost it when she saw the little girl's pillows soaked in blood, as they laid in the bed with headshots.

The police arrived, so she went back downstairs to give the police reports on what she saw.

Minutes after the police arrived, so did Chelsea and she went crazy. The police had to restrain her and calm her down. She couldn't believe her babies were viciously murdered.

Chapter Twenty-Nine
Pink Houses, BK

Stacks was in the back of the Pink Houses projects parked in a Cadillac SRX, wearing a Rastafarian hat with dreads, dirty clothes, chapped lips, glasses and a pair of playless shoes.

It was close to midnight, so the hood was dark and just about empty besides a few people going building to building, trying to get high.

Tonight was the night he dealt with YB. He couldn't just sit back knowing the nigga who robbed him was still breathing and out there spending his shit.

Stacks saw there was a brick holding the door back open to YB's Aunty Bill's. He went to school with her, but she was four years his senior.

He took the stairs to see puddles of piss, crack baggies, cigarette butts, gang writing on the walls, and used condom wrappers.

Once on the fourth floor, he felt disgusted. This was hands down the nastiest building in the project since he was a little kid.

He knocked on Jelissa's door, looking down the hall to make sure he was clear because he knew how nosey people were in this building. They loved the call the police on a nigga for anything.

"Who fucking knocking on my damn door at midnight? Nigga, it better be a big dick with some money," Jelissa mumbled as she looked through her small people to see a man with dreads looking like Pookie from New Jack City. "This ain't no crack house. Who the fuck are you?" Jelissa opened the door wearing a see-through nightgown, showing her hard, dark nipples and big tits.

Jelissa looked like an older Keke Palmer with a gut and love handles, some brown skin, thick lips, cute face, and nice round ass.

Without any words, Stacks knocked her in the stomach so hard, she tumbled backwards and fell on her back.

Stacks walked inside with his 50 cal canon at his side, closing the door behind him. She was now crawling on the living room, trying to get to a phone to call police.

"Hold on, slow down," he said grabbing her by her tracks in her head.

"Please, I have no money or drugs. You can have the food in the kitchen. The drug dealers live next door," she screamed. She noticed something familiar about his eyes and voice.

"This ain't about you, Jelissa. In high school, you were the same way but I'm here for YB. Where is he?" Stacks asked taking off the fake dreads and glasses.

"Stacks," she said, shocked the man whom she had a crush on was here with a gun pointed at her.

"We can be friendly later. I am giving you ten seconds," he stated seriously, cocking his gun back.

"He is across town at a chick's house."

"Where is your phone?"

"Here."

"No, call him and tell him you're having serious chest pains as if you're about to have a heart attack and you need to get to a hospital," he said. As she dialed his number, her hands were shaking.

"YB, please come take me to the hospital. I'm having chest pain and I feel dizzy. What? I can't take a cab. I can't walk. Please, just get here fast," she said hanging up with tears in her eyes

"Thank you, but you should put some clothes now. Have you ever heard of a razor?"

"Lord, please save me. Watch over me and protect me from the devil. They seek refuge in Satan," she said as Stacks put a silencer on his canon.

"Listen, bitch that's not going to save you. At least not today. When's the last time your fat ass even being in a church? I ain't talking about churches chicken," he laughed.

Ten minutes later, the door flew open and YB rushed in wearing a Fendi sweat suit and two rope chains with VVS diamonds in his ears.

When YB saw his aunty being held at gunpoint, he pulled out and aimed his 9mm at Stacks.

"Put the gun down or I am blowing her fucking fat head off," Stacks screamed, with his gun to Jelissa's head.

"YB, please do what he says," his aunty said.

"You caught me lacking son," YB said pissed off as he slowly placed his gun on the floor.

"Rule number one, never disarm yourself," Stacks said as he shot Jelissa twice in the back of her head.

"No!" YB yelled as he saw his aunt's brains splatter on the coffee table.

"Now let's get down to business. Get on your fucking knees," Stacks said walking towards him kicking his 9mm across the living room floor.

YB had no choice as he got on his knees with tears welled in his eyes. He was trying to hold back from breaking down because Jelissa raised him and he felt like it was his fault she was now dead.

"I should make you suck my dick and balls, you bitch ass nigga," Stacks said, forcing the gun in his mouth while looking him in his eyes

"Fuck you, nigga. Handle your business. I ain't scared to die. I wasn't scared to live," YB said feeling the silencer down his throat almost choking on it.

"No worries, I'ma make your wish come true but why steal from me? Outta all niggas, why me?"

"Because I'ma jack boy so if you got it, I'ma take it," YB stated cold heartedly.

"Like a true Brooklyn knight, kid, but you just got off on the wrong exit," Stacks said before he shot YB in his face eleven times. He walked out and never looked back as he smiled a devilish smirk.

***

Bed-Stuy, BK

Tookie was in a hole in the wall strip club, throwing money, watching dancers shake their ass all over the room, as thirsty niggas spent their rent money fronting like they were balling.

Tookie was in the club twenty deep. Since he been home and fucking with Murda, he was able to build his own crew and sell weight throughout BK.

He was moving fifty to sixty keys a week, but for the past couple of weeks, Murda closed down shop. Luckily, Tookie still had bricks left that he was still bubbling off of.

A slim brown skin came and sat in his lap. She started to grind on his dick in her G string bikini.

Tookie grabbed her small waist to see she had four bullet wound marks on her thighs. He placed two blue faces in her pussy, which was warm and gushy, but when he smelled his fingers, it smelled like fish.

"What's wrong?" she said seeing the sour look on his face as she was still dancing to the Kap G and YFN Lucci song, blurring in the club.

"Get off my lap. Go hit the floor or something," he told her, pushing her off his lap as he felt his phone vibrating. "Holla. Who's this?" Tookie saw the dancer mean mugging him as she left his section to grab the first nigga she saw and started to bend over and dance on him as her small titties bounced out showing her flat chest and small dark, pierced nipples.

"What? I'm on my way." Tookie rushed out the club leaving his crew behind thinking about what Ciara from his building just told him.

She said some shot YB and his aunt in a home invasion, but she didn't know if they were alive are not.

Tookie was speeding to King County Hospital hoping Allah would save his brother. Tookie became a Muslim his first prison bid. Although he was on his blood shit, he still believed in his religion.

He knew YB was a real soldier. If YB was dead, Tookie vowed to turn Brooklyn up and get back on his bully.

Chapter Thirty
Brewster, NY

Chris relocated him and his wife further upstate to a nice house on a small farm with chickens, a barn, and six acres of farmland.

Since he lost his daughters, months ago he took a vacation from his job and his boss gave him some time to get his life back in order because he saw the change in him dramatically.

After his daughters were found dead along with a babysitter and a black kid, life been in slow motion. He felt like he was living on borrowed time.

He still owed the mob their money and he knew they killed his family. He could never picture them doing that to Chelsea because she was family and her father was a godfather, a Don, the boss over the biggest mafia family in Florence, Italy but he had major heist in Vegas and Jersey.

Joe was an ant sized compared to Chelsea's father. When he came to the states for his grandbaby's funeral, he came fifty deep and promised to find the killers.

Chris told Chelsea it was a home invasion he believed, and the police had no clue who committed the crime because there was no DNA, hair samples, saliva, fingerprints, or witnesses to help solve the vicious case. He admitted that it would \ likely become a cold case under the desk of some lazy fat homicide detective.

Chris was in the house watching TV. Moving upstate was to really hide from the mob until he found a way to pay them.

Chelsea was out doing some shopping. It was pouring rain outside today. The rain was slamming on the outside window. The wind knocked the power out causing the entire house to go pitch black.

"Shit," Chris shouted as he went into the kitchen to grab a raincoat and flashlight. He would have to go outside to the barn where the power box was located.

Once outside, he rushed in the back towards the barn stepping in mud fucking up his wheat Timbs.

Inside the dark barn, was stacks of hay in pig and chicken coops with chicken wire. He used a flashlight to guide him, but it was starting to die as the light went dark yellow in and out.

As he opened the power box, he felt a powerful slam to his head knocking him clean out.

***

Chris woke up ten minutes later in a small chicken coop, tied up. His cranium was very swollen from being hit in his head with a pipe.

He knew he was in danger. The mafia found where he lived.

Seconds later he saw Chelsea walk in the barn in a raincoat with two hogs on a leash. He was scared for her because someone was in the barn and she was next.

"Chelsea," he harshly whispered. "Chelsea, watch out." He was hogtied so tight, he was unable to move, and it was cutting off his blood circulation.

"Chris, shut the fuck up! Oh my God, you get on my nerves," she said placing the two huge hogs in the cages next to him.

"Chelsea, someone is in here. Untie me."

"You're really as dumb as you look. I don't know how I fell for you. Maybe it was the black dick," she said in her white girl voice as her blue bright eyes, shined in the dark"

"You did this?"

"Of course, you dummy," she replied. "Let me tell you why, Chris. Your gambling problem got my kids murdered and made my life hell on a sunny day. You fucked my life up, Chris because you want to owe money, sniff coke, and whatever else. If a man can't control his habits and can't take care of his family, then he is not a real man," she stated as she squatted.

"Chelsea, I fucked up. I made a mistake. You don't have to do this," he begged.

"Oh yes I do. You know, there is a side to me you don't know. I am my father's daughter. You took me being a blonde and a housewife for granted. If you would've played your cards right, we wouldn't be here, now would we?"

"I can make it up to you, I swear."

"Sorry, Chris, but sometimes you have to burn a bridge to create a distant. You see these hungry hogs? Well, they're killer hogs from Asia. They eat flesh, so I am going to sit here and watch them have fun," she stated as she pulled the latch up as two hogs entered his cage.

"Babe, please, don't do this," he screamed as the two hogs paced around him sniffing with their big noise and sharp long teeth.

The hogs started to bite big chunks into his arms and thighs, as blood squirted everywhere, and he screamed.

Chelsea was smiling, showing her nice perfect set of nice teeth.

When the hogs ate blood and flesh, they went crazy on Chris, snatching out his liver, kidney, hearts, lungs as he laid there dead. They spent two hours eating his flesh off his bones.

***

Three Months Later
New Jersey

Freddy was on his way home as he was in the back of his Rolls Royce with his two personal bodyguards. Business been ok for the tycoon besides his ongoing war with Stacks. His people were being killed left and right as well as Stacks goons.

When Freddy heard about what happened to Chris, he was shocked and upset someone got to him first. Whoever did it, he knew they had to be a professional because all they found was his bones and teeth.

Freddy was texting as the luxury car stopped at a red light. As soon as he put his head down to focus on his phone, two Hummer H2 trucks smashed into the Rolls Royce, flipping it over.

BOC.
BOC.
BOC.
BOC.

The gunmen killed Freddy's bodyguards and snatched him out of the car, tossing him into Hummer and pulling off on the dark street, leaving the Rolls Royce flipped over with two dead bodies.

***

"Mr. Freddy, nice of you to join me," a voice stated. Freddy didn't recognize the voice as the pillowcase was snatched from his head.

Freddy looked around to see he was in some type of storage room surrounded by fourteen big, black muscle heads, dressed in suits standing at attention as if they were in the military.

"Who are you? What am I doing here? This is the worst mistake of your life," he told the man with his back facing him.

"Thank you for the warning but I'm Web. I'm the nigga you and your boss been looking for and brother of Chris, who one of you killed. I hated that bitch ass nigga, but he was still blood so now I have to shed your blood."

"I didn't kill him, but I wish I would of. I swear, you won't get away with this," Freddy shouted as Web grabbed a shotgun double barrel pump.

BOOM.

BOOM.

BOOM.

Freddy's head and neck flew off of his shoulders.

"This marks a new beginning," Web said walking off.

Romell Tukes

Chapter Thirty-One
Albany, NY

Carmilla been held hostage for months now. She was taken to four different locations, but she hadn't seen nor spoken to Web since the night he kidnapped her.

She had no clue where she was at all. She knew was she was in the basement of a house and there were at least five or six people upstairs.

Carmilla's hands and ankles were tied in rope as mice raced around her body all night. All she had was a blanket and a dog tray where her three meals a day would be place like a prisoner.

There was no doubt in her mind that Web was going to kill her after he found out everything she knew. She saw a small window in the upper corner of the basement as sunlight brighten the room.

"I hate this muthafucker," she said referring to one gray fat mice that was always crawling up her legs and arms.

As soon as she said that, she came up with a bright idea. There was peanut butter in her dog tray from earlier, right next to her hand, so she rolled over and smashed it all over her wrists, mainly on the rope tied around her wrists.

Within seconds, an infestation of mice was chewing on the rope in her hands. It was painful, but she knew it was her only way out.

Weeks ago, she heard someone tell the men upstairs to use cuffs, but the men didn't listen because they didn't care.

After almost three hours of mice biting all over her hands, the rope was now ripped so she pushed her hands apart trying to unravel the rope. Minutes later it came a part.

"Oh my gosh," she shouted rushing to untie her ankles.

Once she was up, she looked out the window to see a latch and driveway with two Tahoe parked back to back.

She knew she could fit in the window. She opened it and climbed out with ease and took off running down the suburban neighborhood, as people was looking at her run like Forrest Gump.

***

Pink Houses

Stacks was coming out of building six from dropping off Sondra's monthly check.

He was walking to his Aston Martin DBS in the parking lot, but he had a weird feeling in his gut about something. He felt as if someone was watching him. He padded his side for his pistol, forgetting he left it in his glove department.

He picked up his pace as the cool breezy night when something hit his trench peacoat.

Bloc.
Bloc.
Bloc
Bloc.
Bloc.
Bloc.
Bloc.
Bloc.
Bloc.

Stacks fell to the ground. He was hit in his thighs and legs from behind

"Ugh. Shit, fucking bitch," Stacks shouted feeling a burning pain two feet away from his car

"You should have never killed him. I would have dealt with him if you would have told me he stole from you," a voice said.

"Murda, that's you?"

"Stacks, we had something but YB is like blood to me, so this is business never personal," Murda stated.

Murda knew YB robbed Stacks without neither one of them telling him. One of Stacks workers who he pistol whipped told Murda that Stacks was robbed for a ton of bricks.

Days later, he saw YB with a McLaren 720s, new jewelry, and a new swag. He knew YB better than he knew himself. He was an open book, so it wasn't hard to figure out YB robbed Stacks.

What really made him come to that conclusion was when one of his childhood friends told him YB sold him a couple of keys for dirt cheap.

Murda then knew for a fact, YB was up to no good but he was one of them niggas who rode with the friends, family, and loved one's whether they were wrong or right.

"Handle your business, but just know business is turned personal when lines are crossed," Stack said holding his bleeding thighs.

"Sometimes you have to cross lines to get a clear understanding," Murda retorted before he pumped five shots in his chest and ran off as a car was coming into the large lot.

***

Murda got to the other side of the lot and open the driver's side door to his Mustang Shelby, as he felt a powerful shock to his body as if someone hit him with the taser gun.

He dropped to the floor as the man hit him again, shocking his body then tossing him over his shoulders and placing him in a van with goons inside before racing out of the parking lot.

***

Bridgeport, CT

Web was sitting at his office about to dial a man's number who was the number one on his hit list.

He heard from his men in Albany that Carmilla somehow escaped and he was shocked and pissed.

Web didn't really know what he was going to do with her yet. He waited to hear a little more about the case she was building on him.

If it wasn't for a Rafael, then he would not be in this situation he was in. For him to give Web to the feds, his daughter it must be some reason behind his ill intention.

Web grabbed his laptop and video camera and called Rafael, the man of the year.

"Mr. Web, it's been a while. I haven't heard from my daughter in a long time. Where is she?" he asked

"Rafael you tried to set me up and you sent Carmilla at me?"

"Web, who told you this? Where is Carmilla?" Rafael shouted.

"What do the feds have on me" Web asked.

"Carmilla has everything. The case is fresh. You were making too much money and got big headed."

"So, you fucking snitch on me and have a bitch portray as a good woman then marry me? You went that far?"

"Carmilla was never supposed to marry you. She was supposed to do her job and that's all. Where is she?"

"She is dead. I am sending you her head," he said about to hang up.

"Just like your father," Rafael laughed.

"What?"

"I killed your father. Why do you think I kept you close for so long? Now, you killed my daughter. I will be sure to wipe out your bloodline, dating back to Africa," Rafael shouted before his line went dead.

Web was pissed with the news he just heard but things were starting to add up from how they met, him ratting on him and how close he played Web.

He knew this was the beginning of a new war with the cartel, but this was a war worth riding for.

Web had another situation to worry about as he left his office and went to his guest house surrounded by guards.

***

Murda was chained to a bed in a big ass room with fur carpets and expensive artwork everywhere.

He found it crazy how last night he killed Stacks then he got kidnapped right after. It didn't make sense to him at all.

Looking around, he knew whoever owned the place, was rich and classy. There were no windows or nothing. All he could see was a big movie screen TV that played gangsta movies all day.

Murda heard a door open and saw a tall light skin nigga walk in with waves in a nice build, as if he took care of himself.

Web stood in front of Murda, staring at him coldly. He unlocked the chains as the staring match continued.

"You killed Stacks?" Web asked already knowing the answer because he was watching Murda closely.

Web knew everything. He even knew YB robbed Stacks. He knew everything going on within his empire.

"Yeah I did. He killed mine so I killed him and I'ma stand on that," Murda said unchained, sitting on the edge of the bed. Web went to sit in a chair in the corner, staring at Murda as if he was in deep thought.

"I've been watching you for a long time and I like the way you move, but you just killed a close friend to me. There is only one reason why you're still breathing and I ain't have my men whack you," Web said firmly.

"I'm not scared to die."

"That's good to know".

"Who are you? If you're not going to kill me, then let me go back to Brooklyn," Murda said.

"I'm Stacks' boss, but more importantly, I'm your father Jamel," said Web getting his full attention now.

"You got me confused. I don't know my pops, son and you barking up the wrong tree."

"Your mom, India was my first, Jamel. When she got pregnant, I was heavy into the game, so I had to stay at distance. I sent money, clothes, and toys monthly, but she also said it was for drugs," Web said as Murda looked at him seeing they looked a like.

The two talked for hours. He even told him about his sister in the army who had a different mother, but he was distant in her life to since a kid.

Web offered him a seat in his empire and Murda took it, but Web warned him there was about to be a big war ahead with the Mafia and Cartel. Murda was ready to ride for his pops.

***

Bushwick Ave

Weeks Later

Jamika had to take off from work because she was emotional overstressed due to the deaths of Chris and Stacks. She heard about Stacks' death on the news but looked into the incident to see the killer left no trail of foul play. Today, Jamika was in his shop looking for anything to get a lead on his murder as she looked through file cabinets.

Looking through documents, she saw Stacks had more businesses else were throughout tri-state. She moved the file cabinet because her glasses fell behind it but when she moved it, she saw a built-in safe into the wall

"Damn," she said as it was unlocked. When she opened it, she saw stacks of bricks and money filling the safe. "Can't be," she said shocked almost choking on his spit.

Jamika closed it and ran to her car and grab some duffel bags and clean the safe out. The place was empty besides the few cars parked in the car lot. The place was closed in Stacks' death. All of his car auto shops were closed also.

Jamika loaded the bags in the car and went to check on the other car parked outside. Something in her gut told her to pop the trunk.

Once she popped the trunk of the first car, she saw five duffel bags full of money and she saw a letter. The letter to Web.

"Web," she said wondering who the man was. She had never heard his name before.

Jamika popped the other trunks to see the same thing in each car. There were duffel bags of the money with the name "Web" on them all.

There had to be at least $2,000,000 in each car. Jamika didn't want to turn the money in because Stacks was dead, and the feds will only connect her to him.

She tossed all the money into her Benz AMG truck and pulled off, crying wondering why Stacks lied to her. He was a kingpin, but she was still about to focus on finding his murderer. Even if it meant dying.

To Be Continued...
Murda Season 2
Coming Soon

Submission Guideline

Submit the first three chapters of your completed manuscript to ldpsubmissions@gmail.com, subject line: Your book's title. The manuscript must be in a .doc file and sent as an attachment. Document should be in Times New Roman, double spaced and in size 12 font. Also, provide your synopsis and full contact information. If sending multiple submissions, they must each be in a separate email.

Have a story but no way to send it electronically? You can still submit to LDP/Ca$h Presents. Send in the first three chapters, written or typed, of your completed manuscript to:

LDP: Submissions Dept
Po Box 944
Stockbridge, Ga 30281

DO NOT send original manuscript. Must be a duplicate.

Provide your synopsis and a cover letter containing your full contact information.

Thanks for considering LDP and Ca$h Presents.

Coming Soon from Lock Down Publications/Ca$h Presents

BOW DOWN TO MY GANGSTA

By **Ca$h**

TORN BETWEEN TWO

By **Coffee**

THE STREETS STAINED MY SOUL **II**

By **Marcellus Allen**

BLOOD OF A BOSS **VI**

SHADOWS OF THE GAME II

By **Askari**

LOYAL TO THE GAME **IV**

By **T.J. & Jelissa**

A DOPEBOY'S PRAYER **II**

By **Eddie "Wolf" Lee**

IF LOVING YOU IS WRONG… **III**

By **Jelissa**

TRUE SAVAGE **VII**

MIDNIGHT CARTEL III

DOPE BOY MAGIC IV

CITY OF KINGZ II

By **Chris Green**

BLAST FOR ME **III**

A SAVAGE DOPEBOY III

CUTTHROAT MAFIA II

By **Ghost**

A HUSTLER'S DECEIT III

Murda Season

KILL ZONE **II**
BAE BELONGS TO ME III
A DOPE BOY'S QUEEN II
By **Aryanna**
COKE KINGS V
KING OF THE TRAP II
By **T.J. Edwards**
GORILLAZ IN THE BAY V
De'Kari
THE STREETS ARE CALLING II
Duquie Wilson
KINGPIN KILLAZ IV
STREET KINGS III
PAID IN BLOOD III
CARTEL KILLAZ IV
DOPE GODS III
Hood Rich
SINS OF A HUSTLA II
ASAD
KINGZ OF THE GAME V
Playa Ray
SLAUGHTER GANG IV
RUTHLESS HEART IV
By Willie Slaughter
THE HEART OF A SAVAGE III
By Jibril Williams
FUK SHYT II

By Blakk Diamond
FEAR MY GANGSTA 5
THE REALEST KILLAZ II
By Tranay Adams
TRAP GOD II
By Troublesome
YAYO IV
A SHOOTER'S AMBITION III
By S. Allen
GHOST MOB
Stilloan Robinson
KINGPIN DREAMS III
By Paper Boi Rari
CREAM
By Yolanda Moore
SON OF A DOPE FIEND II
By Renta
FOREVER GANGSTA II
GLOCKS ON SATIN SHEETS III
By Adrian Dulan
LOYALTY AIN'T PROMISED II
By Keith Williams
THE PRICE YOU PAY FOR LOVE II
DOPE GIRL MAGIC III
By Destiny Skai
CONFESSIONS OF A GANGSTA II
By Nicholas Lock

Murda Season

I'M NOTHING WITHOUT HIS LOVE II

By Monet Dragun

CAUGHT UP IN THE LIFE III

By Robert Baptiste

LIFE OF A SAVAGE IV

A GANGSTA'S QUR'AN II

MURDA SEASON II

By **Romell Tukes**

QUIET MONEY III

THUG LIFE II

By **Trai'Quan**

THE STREETS MADE ME III

By **Larry D. Wright**

THE ULTIMATE SACRIFICE VI

IF YOU CROSS ME ONCE II

ANGEL III

By **Anthony Fields**

THE LIFE OF A HOOD STAR

By Ca$h & Rashia Wilson

FRIEND OR FOE II

By **Mimi**

SAVAGE STORMS II

By **Meesha**

BLOOD ON THE MONEY II

By J-Blunt

Available Now

RESTRAINING ORDER **I & II**
By **CA$H & Coffee**
LOVE KNOWS NO BOUNDARIES **I II & III**
By **Coffee**
RAISED AS A GOON I, II, III & IV
BRED BY THE SLUMS I, II, III
BLAST FOR ME I & II
ROTTEN TO THE CORE I II III
A BRONX TALE I, II, III
DUFFEL BAG CARTEL I II III IV
HEARTLESS GOON I II III IV
A SAVAGE DOPEBOY I II
HEARTLESS GOON I II III
DRUG LORDS I II III
CUTTHROAT MAFIA
By **Ghost**
LAY IT DOWN **I & II**
LAST OF A DYING BREED
BLOOD STAINS OF A SHOTTA I & II III
By **Jamaica**
LOYAL TO THE GAME I II III
LIFE OF SIN I, II III

Murda Season

By **TJ & Jelissa**
BLOODY COMMAS I & II
SKI MASK CARTEL I II & III
KING OF NEW YORK I II,III IV V
RISE TO POWER I II III
COKE KINGS I II III IV
BORN HEARTLESS I II III IV
KING OF THE TRAP
By **T.J. Edwards**
IF LOVING HIM IS WRONG...I & II
LOVE ME EVEN WHEN IT HURTS I II III
By **Jelissa**
WHEN THE STREETS CLAP BACK I & II III
THE HEART OF A SAVAGE I II
By **Jibril Williams**
A DISTINGUISHED THUG STOLE MY HEART I II & III
LOVE SHOULDN'T HURT I II III IV
RENEGADE BOYS I II III IV
PAID IN KARMA I II III
SAVAGE STORMS
By **Meesha**
A GANGSTER'S CODE I &, II III
A GANGSTER'S SYN I II III
THE SAVAGE LIFE I II III
CHAINED TO THE STREETS I II III
BLOOD ON THE MONEY
By **J-Blunt**

PUSH IT TO THE LIMIT

By **Bre' Hayes**

BLOOD OF A BOSS **I, II, III, IV, V**

SHADOWS OF THE GAME

By **Askari**

THE STREETS BLEED MURDER **I, II & III**

THE HEART OF A GANGSTA I II& III

By **Jerry Jackson**

CUM FOR ME I II III IV V

An **LDP Erotica Collaboration**

BRIDE OF A HUSTLA **I II & II**

THE FETTI GIRLS **I, II& III**

CORRUPTED BY A GANGSTA I, II III, IV

BLINDED BY HIS LOVE

THE PRICE YOU PAY FOR LOVE

DOPE GIRL MAGIC I II

By **Destiny Skai**

WHEN A GOOD GIRL GOES BAD

By **Adrienne**

THE COST OF LOYALTY I II III

By Kweli

A GANGSTER'S REVENGE **I II III & IV**

THE BOSS MAN'S DAUGHTERS I II III IV V

A SAVAGE LOVE **I & II**

BAE BELONGS TO ME I II

A HUSTLER'S DECEIT I, II, III

WHAT BAD BITCHES DO I, II, III

Murda Season

SOUL OF A MONSTER I II III

KILL ZONE

A DOPE BOY'S QUEEN

By **Aryanna**

A KINGPIN'S AMBITON

A KINGPIN'S AMBITION **II**

I MURDER FOR THE DOUGH

By **Ambitious**

TRUE SAVAGE I II III IV V VI

DOPE BOY MAGIC I, II, III

MIDNIGHT CARTEL I II

CITY OF KINGZ

By **Chris Green**

A DOPEBOY'S PRAYER

By **Eddie "Wolf" Lee**

THE KING CARTEL **I, II & III**

By **Frank Gresham**

THESE NIGGAS AIN'T LOYAL **I, II & III**

By **Nikki Tee**

GANGSTA SHYT **I II &III**

By **CATO**

THE ULTIMATE BETRAYAL

By **Phoenix**

BOSS'N UP **I , II & III**

By **Royal Nicole**

I LOVE YOU TO DEATH

By Destiny J

Romell Tukes

I RIDE FOR MY HITTA
I STILL RIDE FOR MY HITTA
By **Misty Holt**
LOVE & CHASIN' PAPER
By **Qay Crockett**
TO DIE IN VAIN
SINS OF A HUSTLA
By **ASAD**
BROOKLYN HUSTLAZ
By **Boogsy Morina**
BROOKLYN ON LOCK I & II
By **Sonovia**
GANGSTA CITY
By **Teddy Duke**
A DRUG KING AND HIS DIAMOND I & II III
A DOPEMAN'S RICHES
HER MAN, MINE'S TOO I, II
CASH MONEY HO'S
By Nicole Goosby
TRAPHOUSE KING **I II & III**
KINGPIN KILLAZ I II III
STREET KINGS I II
PAID IN BLOOD **I II**
CARTEL KILLAZ I II III
DOPE GODS I II
By **Hood Rich**
LIPSTICK KILLAH **I, II, III**

Murda Season

CRIME OF PASSION I II & III
FRIEND OR FOE
By **Mimi**
STEADY MOBBN' **I, II, III**
THE STREETS STAINED MY SOUL
By **Marcellus Allen**
WHO SHOT YA **I, II, III**
SON OF A DOPE FIEND
Renta
GORILLAZ IN THE BAY **I II III IV**
TEARS OF A GANGSTA I II
DE'KARI
TRIGGADALE I II III
Elijah R. Freeman
GOD BLESS THE TRAPPERS I, II, III
THESE SCANDALOUS STREETS I, II, III
FEAR MY GANGSTA I, II, III IV
THESE STREETS DON'T LOVE NOBODY I, II
BURY ME A G I, II, III, IV, V
A GANGSTA'S EMPIRE I, II, III, IV
THE DOPEMAN'S BODYGAURD I II
THE REALEST KILLAZ
Tranay Adams
THE STREETS ARE CALLING
Duquie Wilson
MARRIED TO A BOSS... I II III
By Destiny Skai & Chris Green

KINGZ OF THE GAME I II III IV

Playa Ray

SLAUGHTER GANG I II III

RUTHLESS HEART I II III

By Willie Slaughter

FUK SHYT

By Blakk Diamond

DON'T F#CK WITH MY HEART I II

By Linnea

ADDICTED TO THE DRAMA I II III

By Jamila

YAYO I II III

A SHOOTER'S AMBITION I II

By S. Allen

TRAP GOD

By Troublesome

FOREVER GANGSTA

GLOCKS ON SATIN SHEETS I II

By Adrian Dulan

TOE TAGZ I II III

By Ah'Million

KINGPIN DREAMS I II

By Paper Boi Rari

CONFESSIONS OF A GANGSTA

By Nicholas Lock

I'M NOTHING WITHOUT HIS LOVE

By Monet Dragun

CAUGHT UP IN THE LIFE I II
By Robert Baptiste
NEW TO THE GAME I II III
By **Malik D. Rice**
LIFE OF A SAVAGE I II III
A GANGSTA'S QUR'AN
MURDA SEASON
By **Romell Tukes**
LOYALTY AIN'T PROMISED
By Keith Williams
QUIET MONEY I II
THUG LIFE
By **Trai'Quan**
THE STREETS MADE ME I II
By **Larry D. Wright**
THE ULTIMATE SACRIFICE I, II, III, IV, V
KHADIFI
IF YOU CROSS ME ONCE
ANGEL I II
By **Anthony Fields**
THE LIFE OF A HOOD STAR
By Ca$h & Rashia Wilson

BOOKS BY LDP'S CEO, CA$H

TRUST IN NO MAN

TRUST IN NO MAN 2

TRUST IN NO MAN 3

BONDED BY BLOOD

SHORTY GOT A THUG

THUGS CRY

THUGS CRY 2

THUGS CRY 3

TRUST NO BITCH

TRUST NO BITCH 2

TRUST NO BITCH 3

TIL MY CASKET DROPS

RESTRAINING ORDER

RESTRAINING ORDER 2

IN LOVE WITH A CONVICT

LIFE OF A HOOD STAR

Coming Soon

BONDED BY BLOOD 2

BOW DOWN TO MY GANGSTA

Murda Season